UNPREPARED

FOREWARNED SERIES, BOOK 1

A. K. GENTRY

BRUSHY MOUNTAIN PUBLICATIONS

ISBN printed: 979-8-9888618-6-7

ISBN digital: 979-8-9888618-7-4

Library of Congress number: 2025904548

Book Cover by Marissa Mueller at MAM Crafted: Instagram @mamcrafted1

Editing by Margaret Griffin at margaretgriffinbooks@gmail.com

CONTENTS

LIST OF CHARACTERS
Forewarned Series, Book 1

<u>Reed Family</u>
Garrett Reed: wife, Barbara; twin sons, Adam and Brett
age 14; daughter, Riley age 7
Mark Reed: wife, Ceely; son, Caleb age 10;
daughter, Haley age 5
Ginny Reed: single
Brad Reed: single

<u>Mark's Army Friends</u>
Pete Flinn: single
Alex Freeman: wife, Erica

<u>Dickson Family</u> (Friends of Garrett Reed)
Robert Dickson: wife, Leah; sons, Michael
age 14 and Bobby age 10; daughter, Geeta
age 6

<u>Johnson Family</u> (Ginny Reed's Neighbors)
Aaron Johnson: wife, Donna; son, Carson
age 16; daughter, Bonnie age 14
Grace Hobson, Donna's sister: daughter,
Hannah age 14

<u>Young Family</u> (Related to Ceely Reed)
Michael Young: wife, Heather; son, Jackson
age 2
Bennett Grimes, Heather's brother: single

<u>Sutton Family</u> (Ginny Reed's Neighbors)
Tom Sutton: wife deceased; sons, Jerry
age 19 and Brady age 14

<u>Holly Baker</u> (Brad Reed's Girlfriend)

<u>Miller Family</u> (Ginny Reed's Neighbors)
Hank Miller: wife, Lacy; son, Thomas
age 10; daughter, Jordan age 7

<u>Speaks Family</u> (Ginny Reed's Neighbors)
Daniel Speaks: wife, Janie

CHAPTER 1

APRIL 10

Toiletries, check. Underwear, check. Business suit and shoes, check. Workout clothes, check. Jeans and a t-shirt, check. Oh, pajamas; she needed pajamas. Ginny reached into her drawer and pulled out a t-shirt and sleep shorts. Everything was packed for two nights in St. Louis, Missouri.

Ginny Reed, officially Virginia Clair Reed, checked herself in the mirror for the tenth time in as many minutes. *Stop it!* She scolded herself. Tomorrow is the meeting. Today is just travel. Letting out a long breath, Ginny zipped up her carry-on and her backpack. She carried them downstairs and placed them at the back door within easy reach.

At thirty-one years of age, Ginny was a veterinarian with a PhD in animal nutrition. She developed her own line of supplements for animals, which was selling well locally and online. In fact, her product was selling so well that the Pure Pet Food Company wanted to talk with her about adding her supplements to their product lines. They were even paying for a first-class airline ticket to get her from Greensboro to St. Louis.

There were no nonstop flights to St. Louis from Greensboro, which is why she needed to make her way through O'Hare Airport in Chicago. Ginny had flown before and knew the procedures, but she didn't like large airports. To her they were crowded, noisy, and often difficult to maneuver.

Standing in front of the bathroom mirror for the last time, something seemed wrong. She normally wore her long, dark blonde hair pulled back in a ponytail and pulled through the back opening of her ball cap. Seeing it down looked strange. *It's just a travel day,* she thought, and pulled her hair back into the ponytail then placed the ball cap on her head. The front of the cap said Reed Animal Clinic. Her long sleeve t-shirt, leggings, and athletic shoes would be comfortable for a day spent in airports and on jets.

Looking at her watch, Ginny saw it was time to leave. Going to St. Louis was exciting. She was proud that her product had been acknowledged by a nationally known company, but she struggled to imagine not owning her supplement business. Well, it wouldn't hurt to find out what Pure Pet had in mind.

Walking back through the house to the kitchen, Ginny passed the last family picture that was taken before her parents died suddenly in an automobile accident. She stopped and gazed at it for a minute. She and her brothers, Garrett, Mark, and Brad, were standing around their parents; she loved them all. The picture made her smile as she walked into the kitchen to find her brother, Brad, pouring himself a cup of coffee.

"I'm leaving," she said.

"Have a good flight," Brad replied as he walked over to give her a hug, "and remember what I said; don't sign anything before Garrett has the chance to look over it. I'm guessing they want to buy you out, hence the schmoozing with the first-class ticket and four-star hotel room."

"Could be," Ginny answered as she picked up her backpack. "If the offer is good enough, I may think about it. I just can't imagine how they found out about my little supplement company."

"Ginny, think about it. You sell supplements to people all over the country and Canada. They're both effective and affordable, and your website constantly has new orders," Brad reminded her.

"But if I sell, I put several people in the area out of a job, including you, my chemistry major brother. You run the lab and manufacturing process. I just developed the product. Maybe you should be going to St. Louis in my place," Ginny said, grinning hopefully.

"Uh, no," Brad said emphatically. "They would ask questions I couldn't answer about the formula. Besides, it's your patent, and if I no longer have a manufacturing job, who cares. I'd rather run the farm, anyway. Speaking of which, I need to go plant corn."

Brad kissed Ginny on the cheek. "Love you, Gin. I'll see you when you get back."

Walking out the back door he yelled, "Remember, don't sign anything!"

Ginny put her bag on the truck's bench seat then pulled herself up into the cab of the two-tone red and white 1969 F100 pickup. They had newer trucks, but one was the F150 work truck for her veterinary practice, one was the F250 farm truck, and the other F150 was Brad's. She grinned to herself, not a sedan on the place. Ginny put sunglasses over her blue eyes, started the truck and drove into the lane that would meander through two acres of hills and trees to the narrow country road that would lead to the main roads toward town.

In her rearview mirror, Ginny saw the house she had loved ever since she could remember. The front was a classic white farmhouse from the early 1800s with two stories and four chimneys. On the back was a large addition with a kitchen, den, bedrooms, baths, an office, and a basement.

Ginny loved her home. She had inherited the house, outbuildings, and some land after her parents' death. Over time, she had gradually bought the surrounding land from her three brothers, Garrett, Mark, and Brad. Only she and Brad still lived in the house. Brad had used the money he received from Ginny for his share of the farm to purchase the adjoining farm which had been owned by the Thompson's, who had retired. He would eventually move there; then Ginny would be alone.

The county roads carried her through hills and countryside until she reached Highway 421. Once on the main highway, the trip to the airport passed quickly. In a little over an hour Ginny had parked, made her way through airport security and was entering the first-class lounge one hour before her 8:30 am boarding time. Thank you, Pure Pet.

Chapter 2

April 10

Pete Flinn zipped his carry-on bag with a satisfied tug. The last four days had resulted in the successful negotiation for two contracts for his company, Flinn Private Security. He would come back in one week to sign the contracts, revamp the schedules and start training his new employees. He was familiar with nuclear power plant security, but he would have to research the security issues surrounding the gasoline storage tanks for the southeastern pipeline. There were a lot of safety regulations outlined in the contract that he needed to commit to memory before he started training.

Pete was thirty-six years old. He had been in the army, worked in the Chicago police department, and now owned his own private security business. Constant training for his various jobs had honed his body to lean muscle. Six feet and three inches of solid muscle made Pete a formidable man. He no longer noticed how people moved out of his way. Anyone with the bad luck to run into him would feel as if they had hit a brick wall.

Pete dressed in his usual attire of black tactical pants, black t-shirt, and a black tactical button up shirt. After checking in online and downloading his boarding pass on his cell phone, Pete drove his car back to the rental company then took their courtesy van to the airport. The crowds through security were light, and soon he was entering the first-class lounge, compliments of all those accumulated air miles.

With his usual air of confidence, Pete got a diet soda and a magazine. Looking around the room, he settled into a seat against a wall where he could see the television, the monitors, and the clock. Boarding should start in about an hour. Looking around, there were no windows in the room, but there were several rows of comfortable chairs, a beverage bar, and a small area offering breakfast.

Pete saw the television channel was turned to continuous news. The sound was low and barely audible, but there were closed captions describing the conflict between Russia and Ukraine and the increasing tensions between North and South Korea. The commentators were interviewing experts who expounded on the various scenarios of impending war. He paid attention to the broadcast, wondering how it might affect his business.

Pete had just taken a sip from his soda when the door to the lounge opened. A security officer held the door, allowing another passenger to walk into the room in front of him. Pete was used to surveying his surroundings, and surroundings included people, but the woman entering the lounge caught his attention. She was tall for a female, probably around five feet, seven inches. Her dark blonde hair was pulled through a ball cap, and she moved with confidence as she walked to the room's reception desk. He watched her thank the hostess for a bottle of water and move to the same row of seats against the wall. As soon as she sat down, she immediately looked up at the television.

Ginny sat down two seats from a man whom she considered to be handsome. She always seemed to be attracted to dark hair and dark eyes. Settling in, Ginny opened her water and picked up her latest veterinary journal. She looked over at him, smiled, and looked back at her magazine. Just being friendly.

Pete liked the woman's smile, so he smiled back then turned his attention to the television monitor. He frowned when he saw pictures of Russian tanks and infantry moving across the border into Ukraine. The network also showed pictures of riots in South Korea which were condemning North Korea. He hoped that none of this would escalate into a large scale war.

CHAPTER 3

APRIL 10

Alex Freeman stepped out of his shower and toweled himself dry. He dressed in his uniform of black tactical pants and a white button up shirt. A utility belt fit snuggly around his waist, and Alex looked in the mirror to make sure his name badge was on straight for his job as a security officer at the Greensboro Airport. The last thing he did was unlock the gun safe and fasten his sidearm to his belt.

His wife, Erica, yawned sleepily as she dressed in a comfortable set of workout clothes and grabbed the keys to their midsized SUV. Their extra car was in the shop for repairs, so she was going to drive Alex to work. She was a registered nurse at a large hospital in Greensboro, but today was her day off. She had a lot to do before going back to the airport to pick Alex up after his shift.

Walking toward the kitchen, Alex smiled as he passed the photo of his parents. As the product of an African American father and a white mother, Alex was six feet tall, had light brown skin, black hair and amber eyes. The next picture was of him and Erica. Alex smiled; he towered over his petite, attractive wife of Latino heritage.

Alex paused in front of the television which Erica turned on every morning to catch up with the local, national, and global news. She knew that Alex liked to keep up with anything that could possibly affect his job that day. Frowning, he watched as the Asian continent was becoming more unstable. First, there were the ongoing problems between Ukraine and Russia. Now, North Korea and South Korea were in a mild crisis, and China was trying to step in to protect North Korea.

Yawning, Alex poured himself a cup of coffee and walked out to where his SUV was parked. He got into the passenger seat of the car and listened to Erica. He tried hard to focus as she told him about her plans to get the grocery shopping and other errands finished this morning so she could pick him up from work when his day ended at two o'clock.

The early morning traffic was light since Alex's shift started at six o'clock. The commute was short, and Erica was still talking when she turned into the airport's employee entrance.

"Got your cell phone?" Alex asked as he gently interrupted her and began his daily questions.

"Yes, dear," she answered with a fake yawn and trying to sound bored. She grinned. Alex was one of those people who always wanted to be prepared for any situation. It was one of the things she liked about him.

"Is it charged?" he asked.

"Yes, dear," she answered.

"I filled the SUV gas tank yesterday on my way home from work, so that shouldn't be a problem. If it gets down to a half tank, refill it," Alex said.

"Yes, dear," she said, sounding bored.

"One more thing," Alex said.

"What, dear?" she asked automatically.

"Before you go shopping, would you do a quick inventory of non-perishable food, toiletries and medical supplies like over the counter meds and bandages?" Alex asked. "If this tension in Asia worsens, I'd like to have a good supply of food and things we use in case something really strange happens and there is panic buying of food at the grocery store. Thank goodness neither one of us is on prescribed medicines."

Erica frowned and became more alert, "Do you think that could happen?"

Alex had spent his late teens and early twenties as an enlisted soldier in the army. When he came home, he worked as an officer for the Greensboro police department. Now in his thirties, he was a security guard for the airport. Through those experiences, he had learned to expect the unexpected and respond to all types of situations. It had become a habit of his to always be flexible and prepared.

"I hope not," he said. "If nothing comes of it, we won't have to buy groceries for a while. But this somehow feels different to me. I can't explain it, so just humor me, okay?"

Erica pulled the car to a stop at the side entrance of the building so that Alex could get out of the vehicle. She looked at him, studied his face, then mirrored his worry.

"All right," she said, nodding in agreement. "I'll do a quick inventory of everything as soon as I get home. I can be at the grocery store before seven and get everything we need there. Does that help ease your mind?"

"Yes," Alex said as he leaned in to kiss her. He opened the car door. "Thank you, and make sure we can survive at least a month without having to leave the house." Alex got out of the car and watched Erica drive away.

A quiet alarm chirped as Alex inserted his namebadge into the keypad on the door. He heard the lock click, opened the door, and walked into a hallway that led to several offices. Entering the security complex and communication center, Alex waited for his eyesight to adjust to the low lighting. Two other security employees, Monica and Bob, were monitoring all the cameras across the airport.

"Morning," Alex said. "Anything interesting going on?"

"No. Everything's quiet," Bob answered. "The gates just opened, and the early flight rush has started, but there's nothing out of the ordinary."

"Good," Alex said. "Let's hope it stays that way."

Alex swiped his identification card and walked through the glass door to the main security office. Bob had already turned on the lights and made a pot of coffee. Alex poured himself a cup of coffee then sat at the computer to read the usual messages from the Federal Aviation Administration (FAA) regarding security risks across the nation. Other than a few weather issues in the northern Midwest, everything was calm. Looking at the monitors, there were a total of eight flights going to Chicago during the day. So far, none had been cancelled or delayed due to the weather.

Alex leaned back in his chair and thought again about the tensions in Asia. He turned back to the computer and scrolled through a variety of national news outlets. The reports ranged from impending war to false alarms. No one could agree. That was good. At least not everyone thought the country was doomed to be involved in another war.

Looking at his watch, Alex saw it was seven o'clock and time to walk through the gates and lounges. The Greensboro airport had two concourses with a large terminal of offices connecting them. Alex left his office and walked toward the entrance to the communications center.

"Anywhere in particular I need to start rounds?" he asked Monica and Bob who were still watching the monitors.

"No," Monica replied as she leaned back in her chair and took another sip of coffee. "Just the usual lines at security and people waiting at the gates. No unattended luggage and no arguments."

"Thanks," Alex said.

Alex left the office and entered concourse A. He walked slowly along the main corridor, checking doors, looking for unattended luggage and watching the passengers. He stopped at each gate to speak with TSA and airline personnel to make sure there were no problems and to catch up on the latest gossip. Alex's last stop on this walk through the airport was the first-class lounge. He reached the door at the same time as a female passenger. Alex smiled and held the door for her.

"Thank you," Ginny said.

"You're welcome," Alex answered as he followed the woman into the room, his mind already moving ahead to the conversation he would have with the room's hostess.

Chapter 4

April 10

Alex entered the first class lounge and walked over to the information desk. After a quick conversation, he turned around and surveyed the area. The room was about half full with what appeared to be single passengers sitting by themselves, their attention on their phones. Some were sitting at the beverage area eating breakfast. The flow of people moved in and out as their flights started the boarding process and new passengers entered the room.

The lounge had rows of comfortable chairs facing the main desk. The woman who had entered the room in front of him was seated in the very back row against the wall. The man seating two seats over from her caught his attention. He looked familiar.

Alex grinned as he made eye contact with the man. He walked toward the row of seats against the wall, and Pete stood with a huge smile on his face.

"Pete Flinn," Alex said, smiling broadly as he walked down the row to where Pete was sitting.

"Alex Freeman! How in the world are you?" Pete asked while shaking Alex's hand. "I guess it's been what, ten years?

"I'm good, and yeah, about ten years! How have you been?" Alex asked, noticing that Pete looked fit, like he had when they were in the army together.

"Couldn't be better," Pete answered, thinking Alex looked a little older than the twenty-something he was when they served together. "I take it you're working here?" Pete asked, pointing to Alex's name badge.

"Yeah," Alex replied, nodding with a grin. "It's a good place to work. After leaving the army, I worked at the Greensboro police department for a few years then landed this job. Best move I could've made. The head of security is planning to retire in the next few years. Hopefully, I'll be able to move into that slot. What about you? What have you been doing?"

"It sounds a lot like your story," Pete said. "After the army, I worked for the police department in Chicago. After I had enough of the streets, I started my own security agency. I contract with businesses to supply security guards and training to existing guards. I've been in Greensboro for four days finalizing contracts for a nuclear power plant and the gasoline supply tanks for the pipeline."

"You handle the armed security guard business, then," Alex observed.

"Yes. Most of my staff have worked in either the military or on police forces," Pete replied.

"Nice. So, where's your home base?" Alex asked, moving slightly for a passenger to pass by.

"Chicago. Still the city boy," he said grinning.

"And I'm still the country boy," Alex replied, laughing.

The two men began reminiscing about their time in the army together, deployments, and stories about their friends.

"Did you ever hear anything about Lieutenant Reed?" Pete asked. "The last time we saw him, he was being loaded onto the medivac helicopter after we were attacked outside Kandahar." Pete shook his head slightly as if resisting the flood of memories from that day. "I heard that he'd been taken to Walter Reed, but by the time I was back in the states, he'd been discharged. I tried calling the phone number I had for him, but it was no longer in service."

"Same. Never heard another thing after he left Walter Reed. It's a shame, too. He was a good friend," Alex said.

"Yeah," Pete said. "It was like he just disappeared. No word at all."

Ginny had not been trying to eavesdrop, but the two men were standing so close to her seat that it was impossible to not hear their conversation. She turned her head, startled when they mentioned the name Lt. Reed. They had to be talking about her brother.

She stood and said, "Excuse me, I don't mean to interrupt, but are you talking about Lt. Mark Reed?"

"Yes," Pete answered. Both men looked at her incredulously. "Do you know him?"

"Yes. He's my older brother. He was injured in Afghanistan, stablized, and airlifted to Germany. From there, he was transferred to Walter Reed. He's made an almost complete recovery. He still limps a little, especially when it's going to rain," she said smiling.

"Wait," Alex said, "Are you the little sister he was always bragging about?"

"Must be, since I'm the only little sister he has. But brag? More like complain. I used to annoy him terribly when I was little and wanted to follow him around," Ginny said grinning.

"No," Alex said, "that guy was proud of you. Weren't you valedictorian of your high school graduating class while we were deployed? And with a full ride scholarship to NC State? He told everyone who would listen."

"He told me he did that," Ginny said, laughing. She extended her hand and said, "I'm sorry. I'm Ginny Reed, little sister."

"I'm Peter Flinn, call me Pete."

"I'm Alex Freeman, call me Alex," he added grinning. The three laughed.

"So, little sister," Pete said, "the last I heard, you were in college. What do you do now, and why are you flying today?"

"I'm a veterinarian. I graduated from NC State undergrad then went to their veterinary school. After graduating from the vet school, I got a PhD in animal nutrition and developed a line of supplements for animals. The Pure Pet Food Company wants to talk to me about them. I don't know how that will work, but I thought I would go see. If they're giving me a first-class flight to and from St. Louis, then the least I can do is talk with them. Unfortunately, I'm going to have to go through O'Hare," she said with a frown.

"Hey!" Pete exclaimed, "Don't knock my city airport! I'm from Chicago. Some of us love that place."

"Sorry, but this country girl prefers smaller airports like this one," Ginny bantered.

"Me too, Ginny. Me too," Alex replied, laughing.

Suddenly, Alex's radio crackled. He lifted it to his ear so that he could hear over the noise in the lounge. He heard, "Alex."

"Yeah, Bob, go ahead," Alex answered.

"You'd better come back in here," Bob said. "We have a situation."

"On my way," Alex said then looked at Pete and Ginny. "Sorry, guys, I need to go. I'll try to get back in before your flight leaves."

Just as Alex spoke, the television programming stopped, and the stations switched to a screen showing the Emergency Alert System. The closed caption under the screen was telling everyone to stay tuned for a message from the President. Then all the flight status monitors showed delayed flights to New York, Chicago, Washington DC, Philadelphia, and Atlanta.

"I'd appreciate knowing exactly what's happening if you can share," Pete told Alex with a concerned look.

"If I can, I definitely will," Alex replied, his face mirroring Pete's concern. "You may find out before me, though, if the President speaks while I'm working."

Alex left, and Pete and Ginny sat back down. This time Pete moved his bag and sat beside her.

"What do you think is happening?" she asked, her brows furrowed with concern as she looked at the televisions.

"It's probably a test or a false alarm. Worst case scenario is that we have somehow been attacked, like September 11. I would take a natural disaster over that," Pete said frowning.

"Me too," Ginny said. "I bet Mark is watching the news closely."

"What's he doing now?" Pete asked with his eyes on the monitors and television in case anything changed.

"He teaches computer science at a local community college outside of Winston Salem," Ginny said. "In his spare time, he helps with the marketing of my supplements. He squeezes me in between work and coaching his son's Little League team. He's a whiz on a computer, and he can market in two hours what would take me a whole day to complete. He's worth every penny I pay him."

"Mark mentioned an older brother," Pete said.

"Yes," Ginny replied. "Garrett. He's a lawyer. He lives and practices law in Winston Salem."

"And there was a baby brother?" Pete asked tentatively.

"You have a good memory!" Ginny said with a smile. "The youngest brother is Brad. He has a degree in chemistry, runs my supplement factory and runs the family farm. He still lives in the homeplace with me."

Pete looked at his watch. It had been ten minutes, and the television still had not returned to regular programming. The monitors showed all flight arrivals and departures from Greensboro were now cancelled.

A beep sounded from the overhead speaker, and an airport announcement was heard, "Ladies and Gentlemen, the Federal Aviation Administration has cancelled all flights across the United States. At this time, we do not know when flights will be allowed to resume.

Please see the airline representative at your gate for further information."

Ginny frowned, wondering what she should do about her flight to St. Louis.

"Do you think this will last long?" she said to Pete. "I would hate to leave only to find out later that flights resumed and mine was on time."

"I don't know, Ginny," Pete said. "We're on the same flight to Chicago, but I don't think it's going to leave today."

The two looked at their hostess. They could see that she was on the phone. An airline representative had entered the room and began to help the line of people who were frantically making cell phone calls and waiting for information about their flights.

CHAPTER 5

APRIL 10

Pete looked at the monitors and the long line at the hostess station. He sighed and settled back into his seat.

"I guess there's no rush," he said. "The line at the desk is long, and this is the most comfortable place in the airport."

"I can just go home," Ginny said, looking thoughtfully at the monitors, "but I would like to know what I need to do to rebook my flight. I may just need to contact the pet food company since they're the ones who booked the ticket. I'm glad I wasn't stranded anywhere like you are."

"I'm not stranded," Pete said, shrugging. "I can always rent a car and drive. There's one thing I learned in the army. If I'm in a situation I can't control, just wait and see what happens without wasting energy worrying about it. Then do the best you can with what you've got."

The line at the desk was moving slowly. Ten minutes after the television programming stopped, only two people had managed to make temporary arrangements to their travel plans. Ginny and Pete noticed that people were getting nervous, talking animatedly on their phones or texting. The hostess was booking rooms at the hotels near the airport for those passengers who were from out of town and stranded in Greensboro. The rest were given phone numbers for their respective airlines and advised to go home to make their phone calls. No flights would be leaving Greensboro at all today, and the airline representative was uncertain when the FAA would open the airways around Greensboro again.

Pete frowned with concern. He had never seen a situation in which both television programming and airline flights had stopped at the same time.

"I wonder if the television is out everywhere or just in the airport," he said.

"Good question," Ginny said. She had been scrolling through her phone trying to get information, but the internet had only conjecture and theories. "I'll call one of the brothers and see."

Just as Ginny was searching her contacts, her phone rang. The picture of her brother, Mark, was displayed on the screen. Ginny answered the phone.

"Hey," Ginny said. "I was just getting ready to call you."

"What's your situation?" Mark asked. "Is your flight on time?"

"No," she answered. "I was supposed to board at 8:30, which is now, but the flight has been cancelled, and I'm still in Greensboro."

"Good. I hope you're planning to get back to the farm as soon as possible," he said. "Is Brad home?"

"Yes," Ginny answered. "Brad's there, and I'm getting ready to go back. Do you have television reception? The TV's here all went to emergency alert screens, and now all the flights are cancelled. My phone has nothing on the internet about cancelled flights or what's causing the problem."

"Ginny," Mark said seriously, "I was watching a live stream news show on my computer. The commentators suddenly looked shocked and alarmed. One announced that they were going to have to change to emergency broadcasting, but satellite footage showed that North Korea launched missiles in the direction of the United States. My first concern was to make sure you were still in Greensboro and not enroute to Chicago. I have one contact still in the army that I'm going to call to see if I can get any details."

"Oh no!" Ginny exclaimed in a whisper. "I didn't see anything like that on the television before it went to emergency broadcasting, but I was also in a conversation. You're right, I want to get home as soon as possible. But listen, you'll never believe who I was talking to when all this happened. Pete Flinn and Alex Freeman."

"What!" Mark exclaimed in shock. "That's incredible! Are they with you now?"

"Pete is," Ginny answered. "Alex left. He works security at the airport and got called to his office when all this started."

"He's been this close? I was so busy trying to recover that I never reached out to any of the guys," Mark said. "Plus, I think the whole experience of being wounded was so traumatizing that I didn't want anything or anyone to remind me of it. I hate I felt that way and lost contact with everyone, but that's a conversation for later. Let me speak to Pete."

"Mark wants to talk with you," Ginny said as she handed her phone to Pete.

Ginny listened to Pete's side of the conversation while looking at the television and monitors. They hadn't changed. The television kept repeating the same message about staying tuned for further information, and all flights were still cancelled.

Ginny heard Pete quietly say, "Yeah. All flights out of here are now cancelled. Did they say what type of missile?" Pete paused, "That would be the worst case." He paused again then said, "You don't have to do that. I can get a car. No. No hurry. I was going to research security for gasoline storage, but I can do that anywhere." Pete's eyes met Ginny's as he said, "That depends on her and you. Here, you talk with her."

"Mark wants to talk with you," Pete said as he handed her the phone. "You may not like what he has to say."

Ginny took the phone, "Hey. What's up?"

"Ginny," Mark said in a serious voice, "you need to get home. I want you to bring Pete with you. I have a bad feeling about all this. The schools around here have just announced early closing. Also, the social media sites are blowing up with information about missiles, cover-ups, another Korean War, and loads of conspiracy theories. This could start a panic. I'm going to start packing. As soon as Ceely gets back with the kids, I'll load up everyting I can, and we're coming to the farm. Is that okay?"

"Of course," Ginny replied. "You know we have the plan. Everyone comes home in case of an emergency."

"Ginny, I really want you to bring Pete with you," Mark said emphatically. "I don't want him stranded in Greensboro. Can we do that? He had my back in Afghanistan, and I want to have his back now."

"Of course, if he's willing," she said, "but I won't make anyone do anything against their will, you know that."

"I know, but I think he'll come," Mark said. "A total news blackout is not a good thing, especially after a news show mentions the word missile. My guess is that the President will address the nation before long. *Someone* needs to address the nation before a panic begins. This is unprecedented."

"People needing flights out of here are already in a panic," Ginny said. "We'll leave as soon as possible. I'll keep you posted, and you keep me posted on your progress getting home."

"Okay. Ginny, bring Alex, too, if he can get away from the airport," Mark said. "Tell him to bring his family."

"All right. Now you're scaring me," Ginny said. "Mark, what's really happening? What do you know that I need to know?"

"Ginny," Mark said, "you know the plan. Follow it. Remember what we said could be happening if a total news blackout occurred and transportation was stopped."

"Yes, I remember," Ginny said. "We can all still get to the farm, can't we?"

"Yes," he reassured her. "Traffic may be bad because people will be in a panic to get home, but you can still get there. If things get too overwhelming, let Pete drive. He was one of the best drivers under pressure when we were deployed. Now, hang up, get Pete and Alex and get to the farm. And Ginny,"

"Yes?" she asked.

"Don't forget to pray. Pray the road home," Mark said. "We'll do the same."

Those words were an immediate comfort to Ginny. Their parents had started the phrase 'pray the road' when their children became licensed drivers. It was their reminder to the teenagers to act responsively, pray for safety, and keep God first in their activities. The phrase had morphed into other areas like 'pray the farm' or 'pray the school.' Whenever she heard those words, Ginny automatically felt the comfort and reassurance she had growing up and knowing her parents were praying for her.

"Okay. Will you call Brad?" Ginny asked. "He was going to plant corn when I left this morning. If he hasn't been back to the house, he has no idea what's been happening."

"Yeah. I'll do that now. See you at the farm." Mark ended the call.

Ginny looked at Pete, who was still sitting beside her.

"Well," she said. "I guess you're with me. Does that work for you?"

Pete looked at Ginny, furrowed his brow briefly, then said, "Yes. That will work. Can we stop by a few places on the way? I have dirty clothes and toiletries for four days. I have a feeling I'll need a lot more."

"Yes, I know a few good places to stop between here and home," Ginny said. "Mark wants me to bring Alex and his family, too. Do you know how to find him here?"

"No, but I bet our hostess does," Pete said confidently. Pete stood and walked to the back of the line, which was down to four people.

Chapter 6
April 10

Pete stood in the line waiting to talk with the lounge's hostess. Ginny was staring at the television screens when her cell phone rang. The screen showed that her oldest brother, Garrett, was calling.

"Hey, Garrett," Ginny said, answering the call.

"Thank goodness," Garrett said, sounding relieved. "I was afraid you might be in the air on your way to Chicago. Are you still at the airport? You know you need to get home, don't you?"

"Yes, to both questions," Ginny answered as she watched another passenger quickly leave the lounge while housekeeping staff hurriedly cleaned the area. "I've already talked to Mark, but I'm still at the airport. I happened to meet two of Mark's army buddies by sheer coincidence. Mark wants me to take them to the farm. We're just waiting on one of them to get released from his job here."

"Good. I'm glad you aren't making the trip home alone," Garrett said. "I'm on my way home from the office, but traffic is already a nightmare. The schools announced early closing, and Barbara is picking the kids up. As soon as we're packed, we'll head to the farm."

"All right. Keep me posted on your status," Ginny replied.

"I will. Let me know when you get home," Garrett said. "We have a slight complication in that the boys had a friend stay overnight because his parents are out of town. I'm trying to get in touch with them. Unfortunately, we won't be able to leave for the farm until they get back and get their son."

"Oh no!" Ginny exclaimed quietly. "That's got to be stressful. Where are his parents?"

"They went to a conference in Raleigh," Garrett said. "It shouldn't be too hard for them to get home, unless they get caught in traffic on the interstate."

"Ugh, I already dread the drive back to the farm," Ginny said, "but Raleigh is twice as far. I can't imagine how stressful that will be."

"I know," Garrett said. "Hey, I need to go. Michael's dad is calling. I'll talk to you later." The call ended.

Ginny looked up to see only two people in front of Pete at the airline desk. Pete looked at her and grinned. She grinned back and noticed Pete suddenly look at the wall behind her.

Alex had entered the lounge through a back door. He caught Pete's eye and motioned him over. Pete pointed to Ginny with a questioning look. Alex nodded yes.

Pete walked back to where Ginny was sitting and quietly said, "Alex is in the back. Pick up your bag and come with me."

Ginny did as Pete instructed, and they went to the door where Alex stood. Alex let them through and into the hallway. Ginny looked around. She had never been behind the public areas of an airport before. It was a maze of hallways lined with closed doors.

"What did you find out?" Pete asked Alex.

"The FAA is shutting down all domestic flights in the United States, including Alaska and Hawaii," Alex told them. "We weren't given the details. All I've been told is that this is serious and the President has declared a national state of emergency. He's supposed to address the nation soon. Airline personnel are being told to help passengers book rooms in the hotels near the airport or rent a car if they need one. All other passengers are to go home. There will be no flights for a few days at best.

"Most of the commercial jets in Greensboro are being placed in hangars or moved to Raleigh and Charlotte. Also, this airport is to be emptied and completely shut down, which is weird and unprecedented. All entrances are to be blocked, and no personnel inside. I don't think that's happened since the airport has been in business. The head of airport security is in the National Guard. He was called to report there as soon as he shuts this facility down."

"How soon can you leave?" Pete asked.

"It won't be long," Alex said. "Only half the gates were in use this morning. All the employees are working fast to get things closed down so they can go home. My boss and I will make a final inspection and close all the fire doors. The last to leave will be the security crew and the airport manager. That should happen in about an hour. You guys need to get going. Pete, what are you going to do? Do you need a place to stay?"

"My friend," Pete said with a smile and a clap on Alex's shoulder, "Lt. Reed has ordered us to vacate the area and make our way to the Reed farm. ASAP. That includes you and your family, Alex. He was streaming a news broadcast online, and just before they went to emergency broadcasting, they reported North Korea had fired missiles at us."

Alex looked at Ginny with a look of hope in his eyes. His communication with the FAA, his boss, and the airport manager had stressed the seriousness of the situation. Now, after hearing about bombs from North Korea, he knew that he and Erica needed to be somewhere safer than their apartment.

"That's right," Ginny said reassuringly, "I got the same orders. I know what Pete needs to do before we get to the farm. What do you need to do to get ready to go?"

"Erica and I live in an apartment," Alex said. "I would feel a lot better not being there if this goes in the direction we think it's going. Let me call her. She can be getting everything ready."

Alex opened the door back into the lounge where the last of the passengers was being helped by the airline representative. Pete and Ginny reentered the lounge. As the door closed behind them, Alex stayed in the hallway and called Erica.

"Hey," Erica answered. "What the heck is going on? I wanted to call you, but I knew you would be swamped. What's happening at the airport?"

"All domestic flights in the US are cancelled indefinitely," Alex said. "If this doesn't get any better, it may be more than air travel that gets stopped."

"I'm glad you had me buy extra supplies," Erica said, "but Alex, what do we do if this is long term? These supplies won't last forever."

"How do you feel about going to a farm?" Alex asked.

"What?" she asked incredulously. "A farm? What are you talking about? We don't know anyone with a farm!"

"Well, it turns out I do," Alex told her. "Do you remember me talking about my army buddy, Mark Reed? Turns out he has a farm, and we've been invited to stay there until this is over. What do you say?"

"I say, when do we leave?" Erica said emphatically.

"I was hoping that you'd feel that way," Alex said. "I have a ride home. You pack. Everything. All types of clothes, bedding, tools, everything. Then box up every item of food and paper products we have. Pack everything in bins, boxes, and suitcases. If you have time, open the gun case. Daddy may need to go huntin' again."

"Okay then," she said hurriedly. "I need to get started. There's a lot to do. I'll see you when I see you. I hope I have everything done. Love you."

"We should be there in a couple of hours. Love you, too, Erica.

Bye," Alex said, and ended the call. He opened the door to the lounge and motioned for Pete and Ginny to join him in the hallway.

Ginny looked around to see airport personnel hurrying along the corridors. Some were leaving, some were locking doors, and Bob was checking safety equipment.

"Erica and I are going to the farm with you," Alex told them as he led them down the hallway. Pete and Ginny walked quickly, pulling their carry-on luggage.

"You'll need to wait in my office while we secure the building," Alex told them. "Oh, and I'll need a ride home. Currently, we have only one car. The other is in the shop. Erica brought me to work this morning. That's lousy timing; I hope we can fit everything in the SUV."

"I drove a pickup," Ginny said. "I keep tie-downs under the seat, so we should be able to pack anything you want to take except big furniture."

Pete said, "Get moving, Alex. The sooner you're finished, the sooner we can get out of here."

Alex opened the door to his office for Pete and Ginny then left to finish securing the airport. Ginny and Pete sat on the chairs in front of the desk. The security monitors faced Alex's office, and the pair could watch the systematic progression of the airport being shut down.

Personnel left, housekeeping emptied trash cans, and the areas were searched. As each area was declared vacant, fire doors were closed, and one by one, the monitors went blank. Ginny thought the airport staff looked anxious and were working quickly. Finally, all the monitors were blank. Housekeeping entered the communications room. Once they were done, the security guards and airport manager locked the doors and prepared to leave the building. Each guard was assigned an entry point to exit and lock the gates.

Pete and Ginny watched as Alex shook the hands of the airport's manager and the head of security. Alex watched his coworkers leave then turned to Pete and Ginny. He motioned for them to follow him and prepared to lead them into the maze of hallways.

"This is a sad day," Alex said as he locked another door. "I hope I have an airport and a job to come back to. We missed the President's speech. Hopefully Erica watched it and can fill us in on the details."

Ginny said, "I'm in the short-term parking lot."

"I thought so," Alex replied, "that's why I volunteered for the front gate. Let's go." Alex led Ginny and Pete through the now empty airport to the front entrance, locking doors and turning off lights as they went.

Ginny felt a shiver at how quiet and desolate the building felt. She was a little apprehensive as to how the men would feel about riding in a vintage pickup truck, because it was not as big and powerful as the newer models, but her worries were needless.

When the men saw that there was only one truck left in the short term parking lot, both grinned and said, "Sweet ride!"

"I like it," she said smiling, "and it has a full tank."

Ginny wrapped their luggage in a tarp and secured it in the bed of the truck. The three climbed into the cab.

"Okay, Alex," Ginny said. "Which way?" Alex guided them to the exit where Ginny stopped. Alex got out then closed and locked the gate.

When Alex got back into the truck, he said, "Take a right and follow Highway 68. We live just outside of Oak Ridge. Where are we going, anyway? The farm, I mean."

"The farm is in the foothills outside of Elkin," Ginny said. "That's the best way I can tell you. You'll just have to see. It's very rural."

Ginny slowed as she approached the interstate. They saw that traffic in both directions was bumper to bumper and slow, but it was moving.

"Wow," Ginny said, "Mark said traffic would get bad. I guess we won't take the main highway. That's fine with me; I like the scenic route better anyway."

"That may be good," Pete said. "I'll find places to buy what I need off the interstates."

"Have no fear," Ginny said with a reassuring smile. "I know every outdoor store, pharmacy, and grocery west of Winston Salem. Part of my practice is mobile. If there's a horse in the three counties around the farm, then the odds are that I've been out to see it."

Not long after they crossed the interstate, a loud explosion was heard, followed by two more. Looking in the rearview mirror and side mirrors, Ginny, Pete, and Alex could see a massive ball of black smoke filling the sky.

Pete looked at Alex. "Jet fuel?"

"Probably," Alex replied. "Someone must have gotten into too big of a hurry to shut things down and forgot a step in the safety protocol." He sighed, "At least the terminal was evacuated. I hope they stop that fire before it reaches the buildings, or I may need to look for another job when this is all over."

"Do I need to take you back?" Ginny asked Alex.

"No," Alex replied. "Keep going. I fulfilled my responsibilities. I'm not on that safety team."

Ginny nodded and continued driving.

Chapter 7

April 10

Ginny felt a growing frustration as she slowly maneuvered through the increasing traffic on Highway 68. She was afraid getting back to the farm was going to get harder as the day progressed. Just before reaching Oak Ridge, Alex instructed her to turn off the main road. Two streets later they were pulling into the parking area of the apartment complex where he lived.

"Go to the back," Alex said. "Our apartment faces a small patch of woods."

Ginny pulled into the parking place beside a black SUV. Alex jumped out and ran to the door. Ginny looked around at the maple trees with early spring leaves that framed what appeared to be a very comfortable place to live. There was a lot of activity in the parking lot as people were unloading supplies from their cars or hurriedly packing their cars to leave.

Erica opened the door to the apartment before Alex could fumble for his keys. She reached up and hugged her husband, relief obvious on her face. Alex held her hand and pulled her out onto the sidewalk. Ginny and Pete got out of the truck, preparing to meet Alex's wife.

"Honey, you're not going to believe this," Alex said. "You know how I talked about Pete, Mark and the guys I was in the army with?"

"Yes," she answered.

Alex smiled and said, "Erica, meet Pete, the crazy driver I was always laughing about."

"Erica, it's nice to meet you," Pete said with a smile as he walked up the sidewalk to greet her.

"My goodness. Pete, I feel like I know you already," Erica replied as she smiled and stepped forward to shake his hand. "I must have heard every story that Alex has from those years in the army."

"Do you remember my talking about Lt. Reed?" Alex asked Erica. "This is Ginny Reed, his sister. We're going to their farm. She said it's about an hour's drive away, but it may take longer on the back roads. The interstates are clogged."

"It's nice to meet you, Erica," Ginny said as she shook the woman's hand. "Please know that you and Alex are welcome at the farm for as long as you want to stay, but I think we need to get your belongings and start the trip. We still need to stop somewhere to let Pete get some clothes and toiletries."

"Alex," Erica said, "I have a lot of stuff packed and sitting inside the door, but I don't have everything done."

"No worries, Erica," Alex said. "We can finish together." He looked at Ginny. "There's a large discount store down the street if you want to take Pete there. It should have everything you need."

"That sounds good. Can I leave these inside the door?" Pete asked as he took the luggage out of the bed of the truck. "I don't want to risk their being stolen."

"Good idea," Alex said. "You guys go on. We'll finish here. Half hour tops."

The cab doors slammed as Ginny and Pete got back into the truck. Ginny started the engine then pulled out of the apartment complex, turned right, and within a mile had found the store that Alex recommended. The large parking lot was almost full. People were rushing in and out of the store, quickly loading their cars, and talking frantically on their cell phones. Ginny and Pete took two abandonded carts from between the cars and went inside, where they noticed that most of the shoppers were clustered in the grocery aisles.

They went straight to the toiletry section. Each had a cart and filled it with toiletries, over the counter medicines, vitamins, and supplements. Ginny added feminine supplies to her cart. She also gathered pet food for her dog, Barf, an odd mix of German Shepherd, blue tick hound, and Doberman.

While Pete searched for clothes in the men's section, Ginny thought about supplies they might need on the farm. She got batteries, flashlights, candles, matches, oil lamps and lantern oil. There were still some paper products on the shelves, so she added those as well. With her cart almost overflowing, she picked out two large storage bins and met Pete at the front.

Ginny watched Pete's eyes roam around the store. She understood that he was practicing what her brother called situational awareness. Following his lead, she did the same. Ginny noticed everyone had carts loaded with food and paper products. The people in the checkout lines were quiet or nervously texting on their cell phones, but Ginny could hear arguments in the back of the store where items were disappearing from the shelves.

Neither spoke. They continued to watch the crowd as they moved up in line. Pete checked out first then waited for Ginny. Together they walked their carts to the truck and unloaded their purchases into the storage bins. They secured the bins with the tie-downs and bungee cords then drove back to Alex's apartment. At the apartment, Alex and Erica stood by a pile of bins and suitcases sitting on the curb, ready to go into the bed of the truck.

When everything was secure, Pete glanced into the back of Alex's

SUV. It was loaded with bags of belongings and a large pile of guns and ammunition. He raised an eyebrow and looked at Alex.

"I like to go hunting," Alex said with a shrug, "and I like to feel safe."

"I know," Pete said seriously. "I keep thinking about my condo back in Chicago and its contents. I hope it's all there when I finally get home." In a lower voice he said, "There were a few guns at the store, but all the ammo was gone. People are spooked. Did you hear what the President said? I saw him on the TV screens in the store. I think the networks were replaying it, but I didn't stop to listen."

"Yes," Alex replied. "I listened to a repeat of it while we packed. North Korea has declared the cease fire agreement with the United States from the Korean War void. According to the news, their dictator opened missile silos and pointed mobile launchers to the east. Then nuclear missiles were launched toward us, but they detonated over the Pacific.

"The President has declared a national state of emergency and asked anyone traveling to get to their destination and remain there until the crisis has passed and negotiations have lowered the threat level. China is trying to negotiate with North Korea but at the same time has said that any retaliatory strike to North Korea by the United States will be the same as declaring war with China. It's a mess."

"Damn, I hate this," Pete said. "Why can't countries and their politicians get along with each other. You know how bad war is. Where are our troops?"

"I assume the same places they've always been. The President didn't address any military troop movements," Alex informed him.

"Come on, you're all packed up, and we need to get going," Pete said. "We still need to stop at one of those outdoor stores Ginny knows about so I can get some decent clothes."

The group exchanged cell phone numbers. Alex and Erica led the way out of Oak Ridge and traveled west. The plan was to use the secondary roads to travel north and west around Winston Salem.

Ginny and Pete talked during the drive about the President's speech and what the events could mean for the future, but most of their attention was on the traffic. Ginny realized how crowded the roads were and how easy it would be to have an accident. People were anxious. They passed two minor collisions, and the drivers involved were outside their cars arguing. Ginny could almost feel their fear and tension.

An hour into the drive brought them just west of Winston Salem. Alex heard his phone ring.

"Yeah," Alex answered.

"Ginny said to turn left at the next light," Pete instructed. "There's an outdoor store about a block down the street."

Alex followed the instructions Pete gave him and pulled into the parking lot of a strip mall with a large outdoor store at one end. A few minutes later he and Pete were entering the store. The parking lot was not full which made Ginny and Erica feel better about staying with the vehicles to guard the supplies. A half hour later the two men came out with two loaded shopping carts. The bags were placed in the remainder of the space inside the SUV, and the four resumed their travel. This time Ginny drove in the lead.

"What did you get?" Ginny asked Pete as they returned to the line of traffic on the main highway.

"Boots, warm socks, a coat, gloves, tactical pants and shirts, moisture wicking t-shirts, sunglasses, sunscreen, and first aid supplies," Pete answered. "I also added to Alex's stockpile of ammunition. I hope all this is time and money wasted, I really do." He paused then said, "I'm doing well with my security business, so I didn't give Alex a chance to buy anything. I got it all. Alex didn't say anything, but I imagine his and Erica's salaries and savings could be stretched thin with this amount of panic buying. Plus, I'm going to the farm almost empty handed. It's the least I can do."

"I thought the same thing about all those people panic buying," Ginny said, nodding. "I do well with the practice and supplement business. I think about that a lot and try to be generous. I hope this is money wasted, too. I shudder to think what this country would be like if we were really attacked."

The two lapsed into an easy quiet as Ginnny concentrated on the traffic and Pete kept his eyes open for any problems that might cause a delay.

CHAPTER 8

APRIL 10

About a mile from the farm, Ginny pulled into a small convenience store with gasoline pumps. She filled the truck while Alex filled the SUV. When her truck was full, Ginny went into the store and bought two five-gallon gas cans. She filled those and put them in the bed of the truck.

"Follow me," Ginny called to Alex as she started to get back into her truck. "The next stop is the farm."

Ginny turned off the secondary road onto Lawson Farm Road, which was a roughly paved road on which the county had never bothered to paint lines. A half mile later, she turned onto a worn gravel drive. The lane meandered through trees and over a hill. On the other side of the hill, she drove out of the woods and Pete got his first look at the farm.

Pete looked in every direction. He saw pastures with black cows, fields waiting to be planted, and the deep blue of the mountains in the distance.

"You live here?" he asked, still trying to look everywhere at once.

"Yep." She grinned and used his words from the airport, "Don't knock the farm, now. We country girls love it."

"This is beautiful," Pete said, laughing. He realized that she had used his own words about O'Hare.

He noted the four chimneys rising above the roof of the historical two-story home. A large wooden barn painted red sat about forty yards from the house. It was surrounded by newer storage buildings with aluminum siding and what appeared to be a covered shelter with one long side left open. Hay was stored at one end.

Ginny pulled the truck into the long pole barn. She got out and told Alex to park beside her.

"This is home," she said to Alex and Erica as they got out of their SUV. "Come inside; we can get the ATV and a trailer to haul our things to the house. Plus, I want to see if my younger brother is in."

Ginny led her new acquaintances through the back door and into the house. They passed through the mudroom and entered the kitchen. Ginny heard heavy footsteps coming up the stairs from the basement. She waited at the door to the stairs and met Brad as he appeared.

"Thank God!" Brad exclaimed as he hugged Ginny. "I am so glad to see you. I was planting corn when Mark called. He told me what happened and that your flight was cancelled. You made good time getting here with all you had to do. You must have prayed the road."

"I did, most of the way, but we had no trouble," Ginny replied. "I want you to meet our newest family members." Ginny introduced Brad to Pete, Alex, and Erica.

"Welcome to the farm," Brad said as he shook their hands.

"We have an SUV and a truck bed full of luggage and supplies," Ginny said. "Can you hook the trailer to the ATV and help us bring it all in?"

"Sure. I'll go right now," Brad said and left through the back door. Pete, Alex, and Erica turned to Ginny.

"This place is wonderful, Ginny," Alex said. "I remember Mark talking about it, but he was being modest. You own a whole valley here. This is incredible."

"We like it," Ginny said grinning. "We have five hundred acres in forest, pastures and cropland. There's also a nice back drive that I use to get to my clinic."

Ginny heard Brad drive up to the house on the ATV. The four exited through the back door and followed him to the truck and SUV. With all five working, it didn't take long to unload the vehicles then transfer everything into the kitchen to be sorted.

The front, older part of the house had a small sitting room across from the main living room. Ginny took the group there.

"Pete," she said, "you'll stay here. This room converts into a bedroom regularly. I'll help you with that. There's a bathroom just off the hallway before you go into the larger den."

Taking the stairs, she said, "The older part of the house upstairs has two bedrooms, a bath and a storage room. Alex, you and Erica will have the room on the left of the stairs. The room on the right is Mark's. That was his room while growing up, and even though he no longer lives here, he likes to keep it furnished *his way*." Ginny made air quotes with her fingers.

The upstairs of the old house connected to the upstairs of the newer addition with a long hallway. The addition included two bedrooms, a bathroom, and a master suite.

"The first bedroom in this new part is where my oldest brother, Garrett, and his wife stay," Ginny said. The room was furnished with a bed, dresser, a comfortable chair, and decorated in cool colors. "The second room is Brad's, and the last door is mine." Brad had a king sized bed and dresser. The room was decorated in tones of red and black. Ginny's room was large with a king sized bed, dresser and sitting area. It was done in neutral colors with pops of color on the walls, throw rugs, and pillows.

Ginny then took the group back down the stairs, through the den and to the kitchen. She opened the door to the stairs and took her new friends to the basement. The group looked around the great room. They saw a large L-shaped sofa, television, pool table, and a wood stove. To the right, one door led to a large bedroom with bunkbeds and another door opened to a full bathroom with a shower. Ginny flipped on the light in the bathroom to show a modern vanity with a double sink and a large tiled shower, all done in shades of white and gray.

"The nephews stay here," Ginny said, gesturing to the whole area, "but the nieces play down here, too. We can shut the door to the stairs if they get too loud."

The wall to the left of the stairs held built-in bookshelves. The shelves were full of books, board games, and DVDs. Ginny went to the middle of the shelves and showed everyone the doorknob behind a figurine. She opened the door into a storage area and turned on the light.

"This is where you can store your supplies," Ginny said. "Be sure you mark everything that's yours. If this doesn't last long, you'll want to take what you have back with you. Otherwise, we'll all pitch in the best we can."

With the tour over, Ginny said, "Well, that's it. Let's get everything unpacked."

Ginny unloaded her luggage and supplies. She took her travel bags to her room but left her supply bins in the kitchen for the contents to be sorted and organized. On her way back to the den, Ginny stopped at the linen closet and got a set of sheets, a pillow and a light comforter. She took them to the sitting room in the front of the house where she found Pete just getting the last of his belongings into the room.

"Let me show you everything," she said to Pete. "When the house was built, this was the sitting room where the family gathered. Across the hall was the more formal parlor. Now this is just an extra room."

Ginny walked to what looked like a couch. "This is actually a daybed with a lot of cushions."

She moved it out from the wall and pulled on a lower handle. A second mattress appeared from below the main one to create a bigger bed. She put the sheets and comforter on it.

"There, now you have a bed." Ginny pointed to the fireplace. "It's safe to use. It'll be nice to have a fire in here this winter, assuming we're all still here."

A flat screen TV stood on top of a long set of drawers. Ginny showed Pete the remote and how to access the satellite TV system. Then she opened the drawers which were mostly empty.

"You can put your clothes in here." she said, opening the door to a small closet. It was empty. "If you need hangers, I have plenty in the laundry room. You passed it coming in the back door. Just help yourself." Ginny paused then asked, "Do you have everything you need? You're the only one out here on this level, so you can move your things into the bathroom with no one bothering you."

"Thank you," Pete said as he looked at Ginny. "You have been more than generous in offering me a place to stay. I would have been happy on the couch."

"You're welcome," Ginny said with a smile. "Mark has talked a lot about you and the other men he served with and regrets he let communication between all of you drop. I'm sure he's as happy about your being here as I am. I think we will be glad for the larger number of people if this escalates and we need to keep ourselves safe."

"I agree," Pete said. "This may have turned out better for me than if I had gotten home. I wouldn't have had this nice of a support system in Chicago. I have no family left there."

"That must get lonely," Ginny said.

"Not really," Pete said with a faraway look in his eyes. "I travel so much that I don't notice it. But it may feel different after getting used to having people around."

"Well," Ginny said, "we're all here and in this together. Consider us your new family."

Pete grinned and held up a fist. Ginny grinned and gave him a fist bump.

"To family," Pete said, "but as glad as I am to have a new family, I'm worried about the supplies I have in my condo, especially my firearms. I have quite a selection I use in my training."

"When Mark and Garrett get here, we can get you a pistol to use," Ginny said. "I think we should all start carrying one now, especially if Mark's predictions about chaos following an emergency come true. Also, I need you, Alex, and Brad or Mark if he gets here, to help me empty the clinic. I have supplies I don't want to get stolen, including some pain relievers and anesthetics."

"That's a good idea," Pete said. "News bulletins on my phone are reporting panic and an increase in crime since the emergency was announced. Pharmacies and clinics will get vandalized quickly if supply lines are interrupted and society breaks down. The crime will overwhelm the sheriff and police departments."

"Thank you for helping me," Ginny said then gestured to the stairs. "I'll leave you to get settled in and go check on Alex and Erica. Help yourself to whatever you can find in the kitchen when you get hungry or thirsty. I guess we need to figure out a system of some sort, but that can wait until everyone gets here."

When Ginny climbed the stairs, she found Alex and Erica stacking suitcases and bins in their bedroom.

"Knock, knock," she said.

"Come in," called Erica.

Ginny walked into the room and said, "You can put your clothes in the dresser and the closet. Just move in since we don't know how long this will last. This is a guest room; I keep the furniture free of clutter so people can unpack. We can store your suitcases and bins in the basement or the attic."

"Thank you so much," Erica said. Opening a bin, Erica pulled out towels and wash cloths.

"I brought these," she said. "I didn't know if you had enough for a lot of people, plus I didn't want anyone stealing them while we were gone. I brought all my laundry and dish detergents. Where do you want that?"

"How about putting whatever is open in the kitchen and laundry room then store the rest with your things in the basement," Ginny said. "Hopefully this won't last long, and we won't need to use it." Erica agreed, and she and Alex stored their surplus items in the basement storage room.

CHAPTER 9

APRIL 10

Ginny looked out the back door to check the trailer one last time. The sun was casting longer shadows across the yard causing her to look at her watch. It was time to think about an evening meal. Everyone had to be hungry. Protein bars, snacks and sodas from the discount store and Alex's house had been their menu for the day. Picking up her cell phone she called her brother, Mark.

"Hey, sis. Are you home?" he asked.

"Yes," Ginny replied. "Where are you?"

"Not far. Topping off the tank at the convenience store on the main road. Be there in no more than ten minutes."

"Is Garrett with you?" she asked.

"No. He plans to come, but he's still waiting on their neighbors, the Dickson's, who are trying to get back from Raleigh, to get their son, Michael. I told him to invite them to the farm, too. Robert is an engineer, and we could use his skills if this goes the way we think it's going to. Hope you don't mind."

Ginny felt overwhelmed. It was one thing to have a large amount of people with family and close friends, but she didn't know Garrett's neighbors.

"Mark," she said, not trying to hide her frustration, "I don't think we can keep inviting people to the farm! We're running out of room!" Ginny closed her eyes and took a deep breath, "Well, they've already been invited. So, I guess it will be fine. It's going to be very crowded, though. You did tell them to empty their kitchen of food, right?"

"Absolutely," Mark replied. "Everyone knows to do that. We're pulling into the driveway. Going to hang up." Mark felt a little guilty about not communicating with Ginny before inviting Garrett's friends. She was right, it was getting crowded, but he was convinced having Robert Dickson at the house would be an advantage.

Ginny ended the call and went outside to meet Mark and his family. Two late model, mid-sized SUVs drove up the lane and parked next to the house. Mark got out and hugged Ginny. He was tall and had the same dark blonde hair and blue eyes as she did.

"I'm so glad we're all here," he said.

"Me, too," Ginny said.

"Aunt Ginny!" Five-year-old Haley ran around the car and launched herself into Ginny's arms. Haley was petite and resembled her mother with brown hair and brown eyes.

"Hey, Munchkin. How was your ride to the farm?" Ginny asked.

"Boring," Haley whispered. "Mama watched the road the whole time and didn't talk much."

Ginny hugged her niece. "People get crazy in rush hour, honey. You know that. But I'm so glad you're here."

"Is Riley here?" Haley asked.

"Not yet," Ginny said, "but I'm sure she'll be here tomorrow if not tonight."

Ceely, Mark's wife stepped out of her SUV and waited for Ginny to put her niece down.

"How are you?" Ceely asked Ginny as they hugged. "Are you ready for a house full of people?"

Ceely, petite with black hair and almond shaped brown eyes, was a physical therapist who had worked with Mark at Walter Reed during his recovery. The two fell in love and got married when Mark left the army.

"I hope we can fit everyone in without feeling too cramped," Ginny replied. "What about your job? I know Mark's campus is closed."

"The clinic is closed temporarily. They will let me know when it reopens. If it does, that'll be a good sign that whatever is happening is over," Ceely said.

"I hope they call you tomorrow," Ginny said.

Ceely laughed. "Ginny, I love you, but I hope they do too."

Deep laughter and shouts of recognition echoed across the back-yard to the driveway.

"I guess Mark found his army buddies," Ceely said. "That's all he could talk about before we left the house. I'm glad they've reunited. Pete and Alex were two of his best friends, especially when they were deployed."

A ten-year-old boy with dark brown hair and gray eyes got out of the first SUV and ran past Ginny toward the house. Ginny grabbed him into a hug.

"Hey, Caleb," she said. "You can't ignore me. I'm going to hug you whether you like it or not."

"Hey, Aunt Ginny. Where's Uncle Brad?" Caleb asked.

"In the house, honey. Go find him," Ginny said, grinning.

Ginny walked with Ceely to the backyard. She stood back and watched Mark introducing Ceely to his friends. Brad came out of the house and joined them. She looked at her watch again and walked up to the group.

"I hate to interrupt this reunion," Ginny said and pointed to the men, "but you four need to unload these cars and park them in the pole barn beside the trucks."

Looking at Ceely, she said, "I need to introduce you to Erica. The three of us can figure out dinner while they unload everything."

"Yes, Boss," Mark said with a smile. Ginny groaned and rolled her eyes at him.

Ginny took Ceely into the house and introduced her to Erica. The women searched through the coolers that had been brought from the other houses and found a large amount of fresh vegetables and a few pounds of hamburger. Several containers of pasta and pasta sauce were retreived from bins and Ginny's pantry, so spaghetti and salad was the menu for the night.

The dining room was one of the rooms with a fireplace in the old house. What used to be an outside wall had been opened to the new addition and merged the dining room with the den. Nine adults and two children squeezed around the dining room table that evening for their first meal together.

While there was animated conversation, jokes and laughter during the meal, there was also an underlying tension. No one knew what to expect, and everyone was hoping they would be leaving for their own homes in a few days. When the meal was finished, Brad and Ginny cleared the plates from the table, and Mark called a group meeting. Concerned about her children hearing the topic of conversation, Ceely moved them into the den and started a movie on the television.

"There are a lot of us in the house," Mark said, "and I don't want the bulk of responsibility to fall solely on Ginny and Brad for taking care of us all." Everyone agreed.

"We can make a list of things to be done and divide them up among whoever is best suited for the task," he continued. Everyone agreed again.

"First, information," Mark said. "I know the television is back on for local programming. The continuous news stations seem to have more opinions than news, which I think is good. Opinion is better than bad news."

Mark continued, "During the news program I was streaming, the commentators got nervous and mentioned missiles from North Korea, but they gave no details before switching to emergency broadcasting. After the President's address, commentators reported on the missile launched from North Korea. Does anyone have anything to share?"

Alex spoke, "All I know is that the FAA has grounded all domestic flights in the country for the foreseeable future. I'll get a call when the airport is to reopen. Greensboro isn't the only airport to be completely emptied and locked. In this state the only airports with planes on standby with working staff are Charlotte and Raleigh. Other states are limiting their working airports as well."

Pete spoke, "I called a few friends in Chicago. No one there knew anything either, except that the mayor has issued a curfew and has the National Guard stationed at key locations around the city. Also, the store shelves are empty of food and supplies."

Brad spoke, "All I know is what the President said when he addressed the nation. North Korea launched missiles, and we're to go home and stay there."

"I called a few people who I thought might know something," Mark said. "All I could get out of the one person I know who is still in the army was that we need to get to a safe place. The situation is highly unstable, but that's all he would say, except for 'take care of yourself.' I didn't push for more.

"Social media is full of conspiracy theories. The most reliable information I got was from a fellow instructor at the college who moved to Maine. He's close enough to Canada to get Canadian television with his antenna. The Canadian news channels are saying that two missiles were launched by North Korea and detonated an electromagnetic pulse over the Pacific just before the apex of their trajectory. The only land mass affected by the pulse was a western Aleutian Island which is not inhabited. Canada is now on alert with no airline flights."

Mark paused as everyone seemed to freeze then began to look at each other with wide eyes. He heard whispers of concern, but there was no panic.

Clearing his throat to get everyone's attention, Mark continued, "That means North Korea may have made a first, preemptive strike against the United States. Because the missiles detonated early, it's unclear what the exact targets were. I don't know how the United States has responded, and I honestly don't understand why we haven't retaliated, or maybe we have and the media doesn't have the details. I imagine the President and Cabinet are discussing a myriad of options and responses with the military, but I hope they'll let Congress decide if we go back to a hot war with North Korea. I expect the next announcement from the government will let us know their decision."

The group was quiet.

"Well, that's more than a little scary," Ceely said. Everyone agreed.

"I think we should proceed as if we're going to be here for quite a while," Mark said. The group agreed.

Mark's cell phone rang. He looked at the screen and answered it.

"Yeah," he said. "What is your situation?"

Mark was quiet for a while as he listened. The rest of the room stayed silent, trying to hear the conversation.

"Didn't know that," Mark said. "We haven't had the television on. Leaving now is a good idea. It could be more restrictive tomorrow. ETA?" Mark listened then said, "Ok. I'll let Ginny know. Of course, bring them. See you soon, pray the road." Mark ended the call.

"That was Garrett," Mark said. "They're coming tonight. Winston Salem has a curfew starting at eleven o'clock. He wants to get out of town before then because he has no idea how restrictive it will become if he waits. He said he'd rather risk traveling at night than staying until daylight. He's also bringing their neighbors, the Dickson's. Garrett's family of five and the Dickson's family of five will bring us to nineteen people. Can we do that?" he asked looking at Ginny.

Ginny felt a growing concern about the amount of people in the house, especially with so many strangers. The only large groups that had stayed at the house had been family.

She shrugged and sighed, "The boys can sleep downstairs. That bedroom has three sets of bunk beds. The three girls can sleep in the great room downstairs on air mattresses. Garrett and Barbara have a room, so that leaves Robert and Leah Dickson."

"They can have my room," Brad said. "I can bunk in the extra bed with the boys." He grinned, "They may need an adult to keep them quiet at night."

"Are you sure?" asked Ginny.

"Yeah," Brad said. "I'll move my things downstairs as soon as we adjourn here. Ginny, I have a favor to ask."

"Sure," Ginny said. "What is it?"

"Holly," Brad said. "She's alone in Elkin. Can she come here?"

Ginny paused for only a moment then said, "Of course, she can. Tonight or tomorrow?"

"Tomorrow will be fine. I'll call her in a little bit and tell her what to bring," Brad said.

"Fine. She can bunk with me," Ginny replied.

"Thank you, Ginny," Brad said gratefully then turned to the group. "Holly's my girlfriend. We will probably get married at some point. We wanted to get on our feet financially then marry. The financial part is that I bought the Thompson farm right behind us."

Ginny grinned.

Mark looked surprised then smiled, "That's good news, Brad. I'm happy for you."

"Thanks. Are we through here?" Brad asked. "I need to move my things and put clean sheets on the bed."

"Sure. Go ahead," Mark replied.

Turning back to the group at the table, Mark said, "Since we have more coming, I suppose the organization of the house and work should wait until they're here. Is there anything pressing for the moment?"

Ginny raised her hand.

"I would like for you and a few others to go with me to the clinic," she said, looking at Pete and Alex. "I want to clear out any cash, supplies and drugs tonight. If we get busy tomorrow, we may wait too late. Clinics will get vandalized quickly for drugs."

"Fine," Mark said. "Pete, Alex and I will go with you."

"Erica, do you mind helping me clean and organize the kitchen?" Ceely asked. She looked at Ginny, "Do you mind if we organize all the food that we brought with us?"

"Sounds wonderful," Ginny said. "Thanks for doing that."

Erica agreed to help Ceely, and the two started by cleaning up the dishes from dinner.

Ginny got her keys, then she and the three men drove her work truck and Mark's SUV along the farm paths to the back of the clinic.

CHAPTER 10

APRIL 10

Pete got into the passenger seat of Ginny's work truck. There was just enough twilight that he could see the fields and pastures as she slowly drove along a path to the back of the farm.

"You have to be stressed," he said. "Have you ever had this many people in your home?"

"Only for an afternoon for a family reunion or a church gathering," Ginny said. "We've never had this many living here at the same time, but we'll make do. Under the circumstances, I don't see how we have any other choice."

"I want to say thanks again for letting me tag along with your family," Pete said. "I would have rented a car and tried to drive straight through which would have been impossible with all the curfews between here and Chicago."

"I can't imagine what a nightmare that would have been," she agreed.

Ginny took a deep breath and felt herself relax. Driving through the farm always calmed her. With everything that had happened, she was glad to be home. While she was not fearful, she was definitely going to plan ahead.

"Look in the console," she told Pete. "There's a pistol with an extra magazine. If you don't mind, would you keep that with you while we're in the clinic? I will be busy inside getting the supplies, and I don't want to be surprised tonight if anyone thinks they can steal the drugs that are there."

Lifting the lid to the console, Pete found the pistol and a holster.

"Nice gun," he said as he examined it. "You keep it well cared for."

"I learned from the best. Dad was a gun enthusiast," Ginny explained. "He shot competitively, and he was always preaching to take care of the weapons. His gun safe is in the basement. I'll get Mark to take you down and let you pick one out."

"Thanks," Pete said. "I'll look with Mark after we get back."

Ginny drove to the back of the clinic and left the truck lights on while she unlocked and opened the door. She asked Pete to back the truck up as close as he could get to the opening. Mark backed his SUV up to the clinic next to her truck.

Going inside the building, Ginny turned on as few lights as possible. She searched the three exam rooms, surgical area, and the general work area with a lab. After she packed up supplies and medications, Alex and Mark loaded them in her truck and the SUV while Pete kept guard.

After thirty minutes, Ginny said, "That's all. I've cleaned out every room, the medicine cabinet, the surgical supplies, and the storeroom. Oh, the fridge." Ginny opened the refrigerator and removed the medications that needed to be kept cool. "Now that's everything." Ginny sighed in relief as she locked the building and told everyone they could return to the farmhouse.

Inside the house, the sound of the diswasher greeted the group returning from the clinic. Ginny looked around to see a clean kitchen with no bins left to be unloaded. A pile of Brad's belongings were sitting on the floor at the top of the stairs.

Ginny tucked medications in the very back of the refrigerator. Walking by the door to the basement, she could hear Ceely urging ten-year-old Caleb and five-year-old Haley to get their pajamas on, and Brad was starting the air pump to blow up air mattresses for the girls. Moving into the den, she plopped down on the couch.

"What a day!" she exclaimed as she kicked off her shoes and placed her feet on the coffee table. "Who would have ever thought we would be in a mess like this in our country?"

"I agree," Pete said as he sat beside her. "It's surreal, like it's not even happening. I feel like I'm going to wake up, and it will all have been a bad dream."

"I would take that," Ginny said.

"Me too," Pete said, nodding.

"I hope I'll be able to sleep tonight," Ginny said with a groan. "I feel like I will never relax again."

"I understand that," Pete said. "I keep worrying about my condo in Chicago. I trust the neighbors across the hall, but if they've left the city, who knows what I'll find when I go back."

"I'm sorry, Pete," Ginny said with sympathy. "I know that must be hard."

Mark came into the den and plopped tiredly into a chair next to the couch.

"Garrett called," he said. "He's about twenty minutes out."

"Wow," Ginny said. "They're making great progress. They must have left at the perfect time to avoid the congested roads. But considering it's only two hours before their curfew, I imagine everyone is settling in to wherever they want to be. If I promise to make breakfast, can we put your organizational meeting off until tomorrow? I'm exhausted."

"I think that's fair," Mark replied. "We're all tired."

"Mark, will you take Pete to the basement before all the children get here and let him pick out a handgun?" Ginny asked. "He's welcome to mine if it suits him best. There are others down there that I like just as well."

"Sure," Mark said. "Come on, Pete. Let's go see what we can find." Pete grinned and stood to follow Mark.

Ginny was just about to fall asleep on the couch when the back door opened, and the rest of her family came in. Getting up, she met Garrett in the kitchen and gave him a hug.

"I'm so glad you're finally here," she said. "Now I can relax."

"I'm glad we're here too, sis," Garrett said. "Where are Mark and Brad?"

"Basement," Ginny stated.

Turning to her sister-in-law, Ginny gave her a hug and said, "Barbara, I'm so glad you're all here."

Ginny turned to her nephews, Adam and Brett, who were fourteen-year-old fraternal twins, and her niece, Riley, who was seven.

"Hey," she said, "you are not allowed to go anywhere until I have hugs."

The three grinned, hugged their aunt, and went in search of their cousins. Barbara had stylishly arranged light blonde hair, blue eyes, and a slender build. Her children all had blonde hair and blue eyes like their parents.

"Ginny," Garrett said, "do you remember our friends Robert and Leah Dickson? These are their children, Michael, Bobby, and Geeta."

Robert, a civil engineer, was about six feet tall with a thin, wiry build. Leah, a homemaker, had been born in America after her parents had immigrated from India. She had an olive complexion and dark hair, but what you noticed first was her personality, which was calm and soothing. The children were a perfect blend of the parents.

"Of course," Ginny said as she shook their hands. "We met once at Garrett's. Welcome to the farm."

"Ginny, you don't know how much we appreciate your letting us seek refuge here," Robert said. "I hope it's only for a few days. We don't know what's going to happen, and I didn't want my family in the city."

"I agree, Robert. Let's hope this all blows over with diplomacy. Let me show you where you're staying," Ginny said as she pointed to the stairs.

Ginny took Robert and Leah to their room then had the children follow her to the basement. She laughed when she saw the transformation of the great room into a sleepover paradise for the three girls. Brad had collected his belongings and was walking to the stairs.

"Where are you going now?" Ginny asked.

"Office," he said. "I should have done that in the first place. That futon is comfortable and the bath off the mudroom is nearby. There's a bunk left in the boys' room, but I decided I want more sleep than I'll get in there."

"Thank you, Brad," Ginny said as she placed a hand on his arm. "I'm sorry you're displaced, but to be honest, I'm glad you're at the back door and Pete is at the front door."

"No worries, Ginny." He replied. "I would rather have everyone here and be a nomad than have my own room and worry about my family. And I agree that having someone near both entrances is ideal."

"I'll make space in my room for Holly," Ginny said as she walked with Brad to the office. "When do you plan to go get her?"

"I want to be at her place just before dawn. She's packed and ready," Brad said. "I want to get in and out of Elkin before many people are up. It's just a small town, but we still don't know how serious all this is. The television news stations are covering the crisis continuously now. We've been so busy I hadn't taken time to even check to see what was being broadcast until a few minutes ago. They're reporting on the EMPs that detonated over the Pacific, but they haven't announced what the President and Congress are planning."

"This is so hard to believe," Ginny said. "Brad, what about the lab and supplement plant? We need to make sure it's secure and let the employees know something."

"I covered that," he reassured her. "Sorry. I should've told you. As soon as I talked with Mark this morning, I went over and had everyone help me shut the place down. There's nothing there but vitamins, preservatives and a few other chemicals. I brought the supplements, formulas and personnel information back here. Supplements are in the storage shed, and the rest is in the office."

"Thank you," she said with a smile and a wink. "I knew I hired you for a reason."

Ginny stood in the kitchen as Brad disappeared into the office. Mark, Alex, and Pete came up the stairs from the basement.

"We were run out of the basement by the mothers trying to get their children to sleep," Mark told her. "Those kids are so wired they may not be asleep by midnight!"

"I know!" Ginny said laughing. "We've crammed eight children into the basement. We'll need to make sure they're tired every night, or the adults won't get any sleep."

Ginny made sure the kitchen was prepped for breakfast in the morning. When she started to climb the stairs to go to her room, Ginny noticed all the men had gathered in the front parlor. They had pulled the furniture into a circle and were talking quietly.

Walking into the room she asked, "What are y'all discussing? Anything I need to know?"

Mark, who had become the unofficial leader, said, "Not yet. We're just brainstorming. I promise you'll know everything. Get some rest."

"Thanks. I will," Ginny said, "and thank you all for being here. I would be worried out of my mind about you if you weren't."

"It's *we* who are grateful to you," Alex said.

"Yes," Robert and Pete said at the same time.

"Well, we have one more to person to get here safely, and she should be here by midmorning," Ginny informed them. "Good night. Secure the downstairs before going to bed, please."

"We will," Mark reassured her.

It was midnight by the time Ginny showered and put on her pajamas. Her hands trembled with fatigue as she dried her hair. Climbing into bed, Ginny decided her carry-on suitcase could wait until tomorrow, and she was asleep within minutes of laying her head on her pillow.

Chapter 11

April 11

Ginny woke before dawn, dressed, and went downstairs to the kitchen. She walked to the mudroom to feed Barf and found Brad putting on his boots.

"Be careful," she said as she poured the scoop of dogfood into Barf's bowl. "I want you back here with Holly by breakfast which will be around eight."

"That's what I'm planning," Brad said, pulling on his jacket. "I'll keep in touch."

"Please do." Ginny said then closed the door behind Brad. She watched her younger brother climb into his truck and leave. Sighing, she returned to the kitchen to start the coffee, grateful for the extra coffee maker that Mark had brought.

Pete finished making the daybed in his room and entered the short hallway connecting the old house to the addition. He stopped to watch Ginny pulling ingredients out of the refrigerator to start breakfast. She had the graceful movements of an athlete, but he noticed that with certain movements she was rubbing her neck and rotating her shoulder as though she had a sore muscle.

"Good morning," he said as he entered the kitchen.

"Good morning, Pete," Ginny said, looking at him with a smile. "I hope you slept well."

"I did, thank you. But did you?" he asked. "I noticed you keep rubbing your neck."

"I slept soundly," Ginny said. "Maybe too soundly, because I woke up with what we from the South call a crick in the neck."

"I heard Alex complain about that when we were in the army," Pete said with a chuckle. "He and a temporary cot were not friends." Pete pointed to her neck and said, "I think I can help that. May I?"

"Oh, please do!" Ginny exclaimed. She put down the pack of bacon and wiped her hands. "If you can work that muscle loose, I will be grateful."

Pete made her sit on one of the bar stools at the kitchen island. "Which side?"

"Left," she said.

Pete began to massage the left side of Ginny's neck, shoulder and shoulder blade.

"There it is," he said putting pressure on a muscle.

"That's it," Ginny said and winced. "That hurts, but don't stop. It'll help push the lactic acid out and relax the muscle."

Ginny closed her eyes and relaxed into the strength of Pete's hands as he kneaded her muscles. She could get used to this. Her family loved her, but this was the first time in a long while that someone noticed she may be in discomfort. Usually, it was she who was noticing others.

Pete quietly worked on Ginny's tight neck and shoulder. He patiently pushed and kneaded until he felt the knots give way to smooth muscle. He lightened his touch to just gentle massage. Pete heard a sound on the stairs and saw Mark descending into the hallway. He didn't look up but could feel Mark's gaze watching him. Pete finished the massage.

"How's that?" he asked Ginny.

Ginny moved her neck and shoulders around and tested her range of motion.

"Much better," she said, opening her eyes and smiling. "You're a miracle worker." Ginny noticed Mark standing nearby. "Oh, hey Mark! Good morning. Did you sleep well?"

"Yes. Didn't you?" he asked.

"I did, but evidently too soundly," she said. "I woke up with a very sore neck. Pete just worked a miracle. I can move my head and raise my arm, which is good because I wasn't looking forward to whisking eggs."

Ginny turned to Pete.

"Thank you. I think I may have to find an extra piece of bacon for you," she said grinning.

Pete laughed. "Sounds like a good payment to me."

"Where's Brad?" Mark asked.

"He just left," Ginny told him. "He promised to be back with Holly by eight. That's when I plan to serve breakfast, which I need to get started on."

Ginny turned and laid bacon out on several large cookie sheets then slid them into the ovens. She was glad her mother had insisted on two ovens in the kitchen.

Hearing footsteps on the stairs, Ginny turned to see the other adults entering the hallway. They all got coffee and either began to help Ginny with breakfast or sat at the dining room table with Pete and Mark.

The bacon was finished, and biscuits were in the oven. Leah was cracking eggs into a large mixing bowl when the stampede sounded coming up the stairs from the basement.

An array of young and excited voices started shouting, "I'm hungry. What's for breakfast?"

A shrill whistle sounded from the table, and the children quieted.

"Calm down," Mark said sternly. "Go into the den. Breakfast is almost ready. There will be no shouting in the house. Understood?"

Muttered replies of "Yes, Sir," and "Yes, Daddy," were heard as the children went into the den.

Mark and Garrett placed a portable table at the end of the large table in the dining room, making a T shape. All the adults could eat together. The three little girls sat in the den at a card table with a princess tablecloth, and the boys crowded around the table in the breakfast nook which sat between the kitchen and the mudroom.

Ginny announced that the food was ready, and Garrett stepped up to say a blessing. Then parents helped their children make their plates, and the adults followed behind them. Just as everyone had food and a place at the table, the back door opened, and Brad entered holding hands with Holly.

Ginny got up and smiled as she handed them plates of food that had been prepared and placed in the warmer.

"Thanks, Ginny," Brad said.

Brad turned to the other adults and said, "Everyone, this is Holly Baker." Brad went around the table making introductions.

"It's nice to meet you all," she said. "And thank you, Ginny, for letting me come."

"Of course, Holly," Ginny replied as she watched Holly's slender frame take a seat at the table. She had gray eyes and long dark hair full of natural curl. Ginny could see how Brad could be attracted to her.

"There was never any doubt about your coming," Ginny said. We wouldn't want you alone in Elkin right now."

"Okay, everyone, finish eating," Mark said, "but don't leave the room. We need to have a group meeting."

"Daddy, can we go outside and play?" Riley asked Garrett when she and the other girls had finished eating.

"Yes," Garrett answered, "but remember the rule, if there's no adult outside, don't go past the barn. You can show Geeta around."

The screen door slammed shut as the children ran outside to play. Ginny, Pete, and Barbara cleared the table of plates. Leah cleared the girls' table, and the boys cleaned up the breakfast nook. Caleb and Bobby chose to go outside while the teenage boys sat in the den, listening to the adult conversation.

Mark called the meeting to order.

"There are a lot of people here, now," he said. "While that's good, it creates more work, and we can all pitch in. Last night a few of us brainstormed about what we need to do to survive here if this becomes long-term and a worst case scenario. We developed a list.

"First the farm. That is Brad and Ginny's domain. Garrett and I will be the primary backups, but we will all have to pitch in where we can. Robert is a Master Gardener. He has volunteered to be in charge of the vegetable garden and fruit trees.

"Logistics of supplies," Mark said, looking up from his list. "Barbara, will you take the lead on that?"

"Of course," Barbara answered.

"Menu planning and meals." Mark looked at Leah, "Leah will you be in charge of that?" Leah nodded yes. Mark said, "We will all be assigned cooking and cleanup duties."

"Next is medical supplies and treatments." He looked at Ginny.

Ginny nodded, "Yes, I'll be in charge of that. Erica and Ceely can work with me."

"Security," Mark continued. "Pete, Alex, and I will work together on that, and everyone will be trained and scheduled for security shifts. Adam has volunteered to be in charge of lawn care."

"Another thing," Mark continued. "I'm going to let Robert, who is an engineer, explain this one."

Robert stood, "We're going to establish a location and build an outhouse. This many people will overwhelm the septic system. Until it's finished, all males need to pee behind the barn. Use as little toilet paper as possible. Since we are on a well system and not a city water system, we don't want to deplete the water table. Water from the laundry and showers will fill up the septic tank. So, wear your clothes for as long as possible before washing them, and don't shower every single day. We will need to establish a schedule for that. Of course, there will be exceptions if during the day someone gets extremely dirty. We will also put soap at the old hand pump in the backyard. Use that this summer if possible." Robert sat back down.

"That's it for now," Mark said. "Any questions? Anyone feel the need to change their assignments?"

Leah raised her hand.

"Yes, Leah," Mark said.

"I don't have a problem with the assignments; organization is good," Leah said reassuringly. "My question is, could it be possible we're overreacting? I saw no signs in our neighborhood that there is a crisis. Now it feels like we are preparing to survive a siege. There was no panic on the roads as we drove here. Is all this really necessary?"

"Leah, that's a valid question," Mark said, trying to hide his surprise and annoyance. He had thought that anyone coming to the farm understood the situation.

"The President has declared a state of emergency," Mark continued, "and North Korea has already launched two missiles at us. As of right now, you are correct; nothing bad has happened in our area. But anyone who works with agencies that respond to disasters and emergencies will tell you that being overprepared is wise.

"Curfews and restrictions have been put in place. People are already in a panic and store shelves are empty. The longer this emergency lasts, the worse that will get. If it lasts long enough, people will get desperate for food and supplies. Coming here now and getting organized puts us ahead of the unprepared people who are going to have to risk their safety to get what they need. If everything calms down and returns to normal in a few days, then everyone will take their belongings and go home. I hope that happens. If it does, we can consider this an exercise in preparedness."

Mark ended his explanation. He felt his face flush with growing anger. Leah made him feel like he needed to defend his actions for coming to the farm.

Leah looked at Robert and said, "I just don't see the need to leave our homes and live in such a way that we are cramped and rationing food like it's already in short supply."

Mark felt his jaw clench. He thought Leah sounded like she was whining, and he could tell she was not happy with her husband's decision to come to the farm. He suddenly felt like it had been a mistake to invite the Dicksons, but there was no going back now. He looked at Garrett then back to the Dicksons.

"Robert, Leah, no one is forcing you to be here," Mark said, trying to be calm and prevent sarcasm from entering his voice. "If you don't think it's necessary to be here, feel free to retrieve the things you brought and go back to Winston Salem. There will be no hard feelings at all. Everyone must do what he or she thinks is best for their own families. Leah, why don't you and Robert discuss it and let us know what you wish to do."

Mark looked around. He was trying to control his anger and also gauge how the others might be feeling.

"Any other questions?" He asked.

No one spoke.

"All right then," he said. "If you are in charge of something, enlist some help and develop your plan. We will meet after lunch to determine what's needed."

Ginny's phone rang. She answered it and spoke quietly.

After ending the call, she said, "I need to go. The Johnson's mare is in labor, and they're afraid something isn't right. She should have delivered during the night. I'll be back as soon as I can."

Suddenly, cellphones sounded with emergency notifications.

Everyone looked at their phones, and the room grew quiet enough to hear the children playing in the yard.

"It appears that multiple cities in the US have been targeted in a massive, coordinated terrorist attack," Mark said. "Large conventional bombs and some dirty bombs have been detonated in Chicago, New York, San Diego, San Francisco, Seattle, Houston, Atlanta and the Pentagon. Chicago seems to have the worst damage."

"Do they say where the damage is in Chicago?" Pete asked, frowning with concern. He had friends in Chicago. Depending on where and how big the bombs were, everything he owned could be destroyed.

"No. The information is vague," Garrett said as he got up and turned on the television in the den. The group crowded around to watch the news.

"I'm so sorry," Ginny whispered to Pete who was standing next to her. "I know you have friends there."

"Thank you," Pete answered and squeezed her hand. "It's surreal. I'm having trouble making my brain believe this. If there's a silver lining, at least these were conventional hits and not a large nuclear bomb with its damage and fallout or an EMP that could have taken out the country's electrical grid."

"I need to go," Ginny said to Mark. "Keep me posted on the news. Just text the highlights, although I imagine the Johnsons will have their news on, too."

Ginny went into the office and picked up medical records for the Johnson farm and her truck keys. Barbara quietly asked her if someone needed to go with her, but Ginny quickly reassured her that the farm was just next door. After putting on her workboots, Ginny left the house.

Chapter 12

April 11

The adults and teenagers stood in shock as they watched the news coverage of the terrorist attacks. No matter how hard they tried, they could not seem to tear themselves away from the nightmarish pictures being shown. The networks showed scenes of fire and rubble in the cities. People were running away from the bomb sites, fear and panic evident on their faces. Firemen and emergency technicians were responding to the disasters.

A collective gasp erupted from the group when the news banner at the bottom of the screen reported that Charlotte had been hit with terrorist bombs. Mark immediately switched the television to the Charlotte station. A remote news crew showed the city government buildings in rubble, and the Bank of America Corporate Building was burning out of control. Reports were coming in of large bombs being detonated in the residential areas of First Ward and Fourth Ward. Commuters had been injured as bombs exploded on the bridges and overpasses of Interstate 277. The devastation inside the I-277 loop was immense.

Barbara started to cry and began dialing a number on her cell phone. Garrett put his arm around her. Barbara's family lived in Charlotte.

Mark, Pete and Alex were searching the news on their phones and began to list some of the places attacked.

"Philadelphia, Boston, New York," Alex said. "All those places have historical significance to the US."

"The Pentagon, San Diego, Seattle, and Pensacola have military significance," Pete said, looking at his phone. "Houston is a major site for gasoline production."

"New York and Charlotte are two of the largest financial cities," Mark said. "Someone has thought this through. I wonder how long this has been planned."

"God help us," Erica said softly. "This is awful."

Alex put his arm around his wife and said, "Amen."

Garrett looked around. Barbara, Leah, and Ceely were spread out along the back of the room and the kitchen frantically punching numbers on their cell phones. He looked at Robert.

"Leah's family lives outside Washington DC," Robert whispered. "She's trying to get information."

"My parents are in Atlanta," Ceely said with a shaky voice and tears in her eyes. "I can't get through to them. The news said Atlanta was hit with both conventional and dirty bombs."

Mark put his arms around her.

"Try texting, Ceely," he said gently. "That may be the only way you can get any information right now. The phones lines that are still in service will be bombarded with people trying to call."

An hour later, the group still sat in the den watching the world as they knew it falling apart on the television screen. Barbara, Ceely, and Leah had managed to contact their families. Everyone was safe and following the emergency instructions being issued by the local governments. With heavy hearts, the group dispersed to start the chores they needed to do. The heavy atmosphere was lightened when the three little girls ran into the kitchen shouting that they were thirsty.

By midmorning, Brad stopped watching the news and decided to plant corn. He was at the large equipment shed getting ready to start the tractor when Ginny drove into the yard.

"That was fast!" he said.

"Yeah," Ginny said as she got out of the truck. "The mare was just about ready to foal when I got there."

"Did Aaron fill you in on the latest news?" Brad asked.

"Yes," Ginny answered. "Can you believe that Charlotte was targeted? It makes me want to throw up. I wonder where the refugees will go."

"The latest report was that downtown is devastated," Brad told her. "The 485 interstate around the city is intact, but not the 277 loop or I-77 going through the city. I hope that doesn't disrupt supply lines. What's really bad is that they bombed the residential areas, too."

"I know," Ginny said. "A lot of people who had already gone to work will be homeless." Ginny collected trash from the truck. "Well, I'm going inside. I'll let you get to the corn. Have you heard what's happening in Elkin?"

"Holly called some friends," Brad answered. "The mayor has declared a curfew from sunset to dawn. All the grocery store shelves are almost empty. The managers say they don't know when the trucks will be resupplying them. Trucks are still moving goods along the roads, but traffic seems to be snarled everywhere. I heard Highway 421 is bumper to bumper in both directions. Kids are trying to get home from colleges; people are trying to get out of Winston and Greensboro. It's a mess."

Mark walked out of the house and joined Ginny and Brad.

"I was able to piece together some more information," Mark said. "Congress has voted to see North Korea's actions as a break in the cease fire agreement of 1953, so we are officially at war again with

North Korea. At last count, a total of twenty cities, and the Pentagon were hit with bombs. They included large numbers of conventional bombs and dirty bombs, but no large nuclear bombs, thank goodness. A whole bunch of fringe terrorist groups are taking credit for the attacks in the US. North Korea is taking credit, too. Evidently, those EMPs they detonated were to get our attention and take our minds off local issues. It worked. Nobody saw these terrorist attacks coming. Oh, yeah, and the stock market has crashed."

Ginny felt her stomach clench. "Well, there goes the retirement fund. I hope it bounces back. Did you hear what the government is going to do?"

"Not yet," Mark answered. "That will be up to the President, the Secretary of Defense, and Congress. I think we're lucky to get the news we have. People are going to stop going to work so they can take care of their families, and that includes reporters."

"What did Robert and Leah decide to do?" Ginny asked.

"They're going to stay," Mark said, feeling his anger with Leah return. "Robert convinced Leah it was best, especially after Chicago and the other cities were hit with dirty bombs. Besides, their kids rebelled. They didn't want to leave the farm."

"Okay," Ginny said. "I just don't think it's good to have someone here who doesn't want to be here. That can cause problems."

"I agree," Mark replied. "Robert's grateful to be here. I just hope he can calm Leah down and help her see that being here is a good thing."

"Yeah," Ginny sighed. "I'm going inside. I'm thirsty and in need of a shower and food. Who's fixing lunch?"

"Ceely and Holly have that covered," Mark said. "The others are doing inventory. Robert has the boys in the garden, then they're going to lay out the foundations for the outhouse. Pete and Alex are walking the farm. After lunch, Pete, Alex, Robert and I are going to the lumber yard outside Elkin for supplies."

"Let me know when you leave," Ginny said as she turned and

walked to the house.

The mudroom had a door that led to a laundry area and a bathroom. Ginny put her clothes in the washing machine and showered. When finished, she dressed in the gym shorts and t-shirt she kept in the bathroom. Robert and the boys were coming through the back door as she was leaving the laundry room.

"Robert," she said. Robert stopped.

"I have an idea," she said. "Could you build an outdoor shower too? Just in case we lose power for extended periods. Nothing large, just a wooden enclosure on slats would work. When it's warm some of us could use it with solar showers. We have quite a few of those in the basement."

"That's a good idea. Where do you want it?" he asked.

"Maybe somewhere sunny? But out of site of the upstairs windows or the barn loft," Ginny suggested.

"I'll lay out the dimensions on paper and get the supplies when we go into town," he said. "We can decide on the location after that."

"When are you going for the lumber?" Ginny asked.

"After lunch," he replied.

"Okay," she said. "I'll give Mark my credit card for the store. They probably remember him, but they know me. I take care of the manager's horses."

"You know everyone around, I bet," Robert said, smiling.

"Just about," Ginny replied. "I'm one of the few veterinarians in three counties willing to make house calls. That's a bigger business than the clinic."

"I'm sure," he said, then hesitated. "Ginny, I understand you weren't asked if our family could come, that Mark and Garrett made that decision without consulting you. I'm very sorry about that, but I'm still very grateful to be here. Thank you for not turning us away."

"Don't worry, Robert," Ginny reassured him. "It will be all right."

Ginny watched Robert walk through the den and disappear up the stairs. She felt better about his family being at the farm. Mark and Garrett had been right. Robert's skills were valuable, and his whole family was pitching in to work. She hoped that Leah would adjust and they could all become good friends.

Ginny stepped aside as the rest of the men and boys entered the house. Riley, Haley, and Geeta came running inside and demanded her attention.

"Aunt Ginny!" Riley shouted.

"What is it?" Ginny asked, matching their excitement.

"Uncle Brad put us three in charge of the chickens!" she exclaimed.

"He did?" Ginny asked.

"Yes!" Riley exclaimed. "He gave us each a basket for eggs. We're supposed to use a special measuring cup and feed them in the morning and at night. We let them out of their house in the mornings and put them back at night. He says it is real important!"

"He's right, girls," Ginny said. "It's one of the most important jobs on the farm. If we take good care of the chickens, they will give us lots of eggs to eat. Thank you for being smart enough to take that job."

"You're welcome!" they all said together and ran into the den. Ginny watched them, wishing she had their energy. To them this was all a big adventure. She hoped they could continue to see things that way.

Ginny walked into the kitchen to find Ceely arranging meats, cheese, and lettuce on trays. Holly was searching the refrigerator for condiments.

"That looks great," she said. "Thank you."

"You're welcome." Ceely said. "How's the horse?"

"Delivered," Ginny answered. "A cute little filly. The owner is paying me in milk, butter, and cheese from his farm. Donna, his wife, makes the best butter and cheese. It's better than anything I can buy at the grocery store. I don't know how she does it."

"Wonderful," answered Ceely. "I heard from a friend in Winston that all the stores are out of fresh produce and dairy products, so that will be a blessing."

"The Johnson's are on the farm next to us on the south side," Ginny said. "I had forgotten how close to the road their house is. I got a little nervous whenever a car drove by, especially after everything that happened this morning."

"I love that your house isn't visible from the road," Ceely said.

"True," Ginny replied, "but all the locals know we're here. I need to talk to Pete about that. I have an idea to run past him. But for now, I'm going to get a drink and just sit for a minute unless y'all need my help."

"Nope. Go sit," Ceely said. "I imagine birthing horses is tiring."

"The mares do all the work," Ginny said with a grin. "This one was easy."

Ginny poured herself a glass of her favorite carbonated soda and sat on the couch. She sipped it, sighed, and wondered how long before they ran out of those delightful bubbles.

CHAPTER 13

APRIL 11

Alex and Pete walked the eastern and southern perimeters of the farm before they stopped and headed back to the house for lunch. They wanted to see the area where they were now living, determine its size, and decide where to put the game cameras they had. When they entered the house, Alex went to the basement to find Erica. Pete stopped in the kitchen for a glass of water.

Ginny stood in the den with the little girls. Her shorts emphasized the muscles in her legs, and the T-shirt did little to hide her curves. Realizing he was staring, Pete took his glass, sat at the kitchen island, and tried to analyze what he was feeling. In all his travels, no woman had caught his eye the way Ginny did. She was smart, beautiful, fit, generous, and kind.

Pete honestly thought he had never met another woman with all those qualities at the same time. While he had never hesitated to ask a woman out, he was uncertain about Ginny. They were virtually trapped together, at her place, with her family for an unknown amount of time. If he approached her and things didn't go well, they would both be miserable.

That settles it. No matter how attracted he was to her, it would not do to act on it. It was better to ignore it. He had made up his mind when Ginny came into the kitchen and sat on the barstool next to him. Pete felt his stomach flutter and his heart race. Great. That decision just flew out the window.

"Pete," she said. "I have a favor to ask."

"And what would that be?" he asked, fidgeting with his glass of water.

"It's about the Johnsons on the next farm," she said. "While I was there delivering their foal, I noticed how close their house is to the road. I sort of offered your services to look at their place and give them some suggestions for security." Ginny gave him a sheepish look that he found adorable. There was no way he could say no.

"All right," he said. "I'll go, but you'll have to go with me. They don't know me, and you can introduce us."

"Thank you. Does tomorrow morning sound okay?" she asked.

"How about tomorrow afternoon," he said. "Alex and I are planning to walk the other half of the perimeter in the morning. Mark gave us a copy of the aerial photo. You could say it's all in the name of security, but Alex and I are just fascinated with the whole place. It's a beautiful farm."

"Thank you," Ginny said. "I agree; I can't imagine anywhere more beautiful than here. I'll call Aaron and let him know we're coming tomorrow." Ginny placed her hand on his arm, "I really do appreciate this, Pete. The Johnsons are good friends and neighbors. Besides, they're paying me in dairy products for the services this morning. Not a bad day's work. It's probably better than cash right now."

Pete laughed. "You're right about that."

Ginny loved Pete's laugh. It was infectious, male, and pleasantly baritone. Without realizing it, she squeezed his arm and smiled before getting up.

Pete had been all too aware of Ginny's hand on his arm. When she squeezed it, she squeezed the inside of his chest. He was in over his head, and he knew it. It was going to be a long crisis.

After lunch Mark hooked the trailer to the farm truck and climbed into the driver's seat. Pete took the passenger's seat while Robert and Alex took the two back seats. The drive to the lumber yard was uneventful. There was little traffic, and the parking lot was almost empty. This lumber yard was local and on the opposite side of town from the large home improvement store where lumber was also sold. When they arrived, Pete stayed with the truck and trailer while the other three went inside.

Pete watched the parking lot. It was only day two of the crisis, and things were still calm. By tomorrow, people would begin to worry and wonder how long this would last. If grocery trucks had not made deliveries, people would start to get agitated. By day four, some would be desperate because they were beginning to run out of food. Across the road was a farm and garden store. He would suggest they stop there before going back to the farm.

Thirty minutes later Mark exited the store and walked back to the truck.

"We need to pull under the shelter and load what we bought," Mark said, looking at Pete.

Pete got back into the truck and continued to watch the parking lot while Mark drove. When they reached the door, Pete stood on the parking lot side of the truck while the other three loaded the trailer with lumber, plywood, shingles, concrete blocks, concrete mix and assorted nails. With the load covered and secured, the four got back into the truck, and Mark started the engine.

"Should we stop at that farm store across the road?" Pete asked. "They may have things we should stock up on."

"Good idea," Mark said, and drove across the road into the parking lot.

As before, Pete stayed with the trailer while the other three went inside. The parking lot had only three other vehicles in it and was quiet. Pete heard a loud motor and car stereo loudly playing music on the street that ran by the store. An old light blue truck drove past with the bed full of older teen boys. They were singing to the loud music, whistling and yelling at people. The truck was weaving in the lane. He was sure they were drunk and looking for either trouble or a party.

They stopped at the traffic light. Pete went behind the truck where they couldn't see him and tried to memorize each face he could see. Something told him these boys might be trouble in the coming weeks. Schools were closed, and bored teenagers could create choas. Maybe Holly or Brad would know who they were. He would have to ask.

Thirty minutes later Mark walked out of the store and climbed into the driver's seat of the truck. The same procedure occurred. Pete watched the parking lot, and the others loaded chicken feed, dog food, seeds, and other miscellaneous supplies. With everything secured and no more room in the trailer or the bed of the truck, the four men traveled back to the farm.

When they arrived, Robert gathered the boys to help unload the trailer. The lumber and building supplies were placed in a storage shed along with the chicken feed, dog food, and seeds for the garden. Two dozen pairs of work gloves in various sizes were taken into the house as well as paper products and duct tape. The baling supplies, extra hoes, tools, and shovels were taken out to the equipment shed.

The men took a break, found Brad and walked to the front porch of the house to discuss their outing in reference to security for the coming days. On his way to the porch, Pete saw Holly and walked over to ask her about the boys in the truck.

"Holly," Pete said.

"Yes, Sir?" she answered, holding a basket of dirty laundry.

"It's Pete," he said grinning. "It'll take you a couple days to get us all straight, I imagine."

Holly grinned and nodded.

"When we were in town, I saw an old blue truck full of guys who looked to be in their late teens or early twenties, riding around with the stereo blaring, singing, and shouting at people," Pete told her. "The motor was loud, and I'm pretty sure they were drinking. Do you know of any one in town that would fit that description?"

Holly grimaced and rolled her eyes. "Yes. That would be Blake Larkin's truck. Probably with him were his two brothers, Dan and Greg. I would bet his two cousins, Jake and Paul Larkin, were with him, too. Blake's cousins are still in high school. Blake, Dan and Greg are older. They're twenty and twenty-two. Those three were behind me a year or two in school, but everyone knew them. They cared for nothing except drinking and making trouble. I stayed away from them, but some of my friends thought they were cool. They just scared me."

"Do you know if they ever leave town and travel the back roads like the one we're living on, or do they mostly cruise the city?" Pete asked.

"I don't know, sorry," Holly replied.

"No, don't be sorry," he said. "You've helped me a lot. Thank you for the information. With those punks in town, I'm glad you're out here. I know Brad is."

"Thank you," Holly replied. "I need to put this basket in the laundry room and get back to the basement. That storage room is packed! Inventory is taking forever, which is good. I'm not complaining. The longer it takes means we have a larger supply of what we need." Holly walked on and Pete turned to walk out to the porch.

"Everything all right, Pete?" Mark asked when Pete sat on one of the porch chairs.

"Yes. I was just looking for information," Pete said and proceeded to tell them about the truck of boys in town and what Holly said about them.

CHAPTER 14

APRIL 11

After dinner, Mark called a group meeting and asked for updates. Leah reported that food had been inventoried. Menus and kitchen work schedules were planned for two weeks. Barbara reported that everything in the storage rooms had been inventoried. Alex reported on the first half of the perimeter walk around the farm and ideas for security.

"Anything else to report?" Mark asked.

Ginny raised her hand and said, "If mail stops running, I think we should take up the mailbox and plant shrubs or trees along the road. It would help to camouflage the drive. Everyone around here knows us, but if things get worse, people coming out of the cities who might venture this far off the main road won't."

"That's a good idea," Pete said, "but I think it can wait for a few days. I hope things don't get that bad. I didn't go into the stores this afternoon, but was the merchandise getting thin or was there plenty on the shelves? Should we make another run into town for things we may need down the road? Considering the scale of these terrorist attacks, I don't see the state of emergency being lifted for a while. The supply chain could be severely affected."

"We inventoried everything in the basement," Barbara said, handing Mark a piece of paper. "I have a list of things we are low on and should probably get while we can."

"Thank you," said Mark. "We'll go back into town tomorrow." Mark looked at the list.

"Pete, Alex, Brad and I will go, but we will need one of the ladies to go with us," he said holding the list. "I have no idea what some of these things are."

The women laughed.

"I'll go," Ginny said. "I can get everything on that list plus a few extra over-the-counter supplies we might want to have on hand. Colds, flu, headaches, and muscle pains wait for no crisis."

"That covers everything, I think. Anything else we need to go over?" Mark asked.

Adam raised his hand. "I've been watching the news on the internet. A lot of our news networks are offline from the attacks. Winston Salem is still operating their TV station, but even they're having trouble getting accurate information from across the nation. What I was able to find out indicates that everything is in chaos with Russia, Ukraine, China, North Korea and South Korea.

"I did hear there is a lot of disatisfaction with our government because of the attacks and not retaliating against whoever did them. Some commentators think there is a state of confusion in the government about who to blame for the bombs in so many cities. Every terrorist group claiming responsibility seems to have a connection to either Iran, Russia or China. But most commentators are critical of the President's lack of retaliation or any concrete plan to protect the United States."

Adam continued, "Winston Salem reported that the bombed cities are having trouble getting to the wounded because of the extent of the destruction and in some cases, radiation. Fallout is minimal because most of it stayed close to the ground rather than being expelled high into the atmosphere. Washington DC is on lockdown, and the area around the Pentagon is blocked off. Anyone can leave, but if you do, you can't return."

Ginny's phone rang. "This is Doctor Reed." She paused. "Of course, I'll come. Give me about a half hour. Where is she?" Ginny listened. "Ok, I'll pull down to the barn. You can show me the way from there. Be there soon."

"I have to go," Ginny said, getting up from the table. "The Sutton's have a cow that calved but the uterus has prolapsed. I may be gone a while. It depends on whether I can get it to stay in on its own, or I need to remove it."

"Is it safe to go?" asked Leah.

"I go out at all hours. It'll be fine," Ginny answered.

"I'll ride with you," Pete said.

"You don't need to,"Ginny said. "This could be an easy visit or take all night. There won't be anything for you to do."

"I'll sleep in the truck," he said. "You and Mr. Sutton can take care of the cow. Then I'll drive you back."

Ginny started to speak, but Pete stood and said, "Well, let's go. You aren't going to change my mind."

"Fine!" Ginny said in exasperation and went to put on her work clothes and boots.

"Thanks, Pete," Mark said. "She's probably right. It's just next door, but it's dark, and we have no idea what could happen."

"No problem." Pete answered and went to his room to change shoes.

Pete helped Ginny hook the enclosed trailer that had surgical supplies for large animals to her truck.

"You didn't have to come, Pete," she said.

"I know, but these aren't normal times," he said. "Anybody who knows you will know you have strong medications in your trailer. Is your handgun in the truck?"

"Yes," Ginny answered briskley as she got into the truck. She didn't mean to sound rude, but she wasn't used to someone else telling her how to respond to her emergency calls. "Why?"

"Good," he said, tapping the holster on his belt. "We have two weapons, then. Just being safe."

Ginny was quiet and felt her annoyance disappear.

"Thank you, Pete," she said in a softer tone as she drove around the shed to the driveway. "You're right. These aren't normal times. I appreciate your concern."

"You're welcome," Pete answered with a soft smile. "You know how important you are to everyone, even me."

Ginny was glad it was dark and that Pete could not see her reaction to his words. No man had ever told her that she was important to him except her brothers and her father. She felt a response in her chest she had never felt before.

Now why had he said that, Pete thought with a grimace. The words just came out. He was glad it was dark, and Ginny couldn't see his cheeks darken at his own words. It had been true, but he hadn't planned on saying or doing anything that could make things awkward between them. He was glad when she pulled into a driveway because now the conversation would have to change.

CHAPTER 15

APRIL 11

Tom Sutton's narrow frame met Ginny at the barn. He was slightly below six feet tall, and his wide brimmed straw hat hid the fact that most of his hair was already gone.

Ginny stopped and rolled down her window as Tom approached her truck.

"Where is she?" Ginny asked.

"I got her in a treatment chute down in the pasture," Tom replied. He pointed to the truck and trailer. "Will that make it through the mud and soft grass?"

"Yes, Sir," Ginnny answered, grinning. "It's sturdy with four-wheel drive, and the trailer has a special suspension with all terrain tires."

"Sounds like you thought of everything," Tom said. "Follow me."

Tom got on a four-wheeler and started down a farm lane.

"Hold on," Ginny said to Pete. "This is going to be bumpy."

Tom led Ginny to a pasture that bordered a creek. His son, Brady, held a flashlight over the cow that had been immobilized in a cattle chute. Ginny parked behind the cow and got out of the truck.

"Hello, Tom," Ginny said as she walked over and shook his hand.

"This is Pete," Ginny said pointing to Pete. "He's a friend of Mark's and staying with us for a while. He's from Chicago."

Tom shook Pete's hand. "Nice to meet ya, Pete. I'm real sorry about Chicago getting bombed; I'm glad you weren't there this morning. All this is just awful. I'm not sure how to feel about it since it's so far removed from us. Even Charlotte feels far away."

"Thank you, Tom," Pete replied. "I know what you mean. It all seems so surreal. I came with Ginny to help, although I can't do any more than hold a light."

Ginny opened the back of the trailer. "If you men will take these lamps, set them up around the mama so I can see with no shadows."

Once the lights were in place, Ginny put on a plastic gown, plastic boot covers and latex gloves that went all the way to her shoulders. She washed the prolapsed uterus with a saline solution, making sure there were no traces of grass and dirt. Once that was done, she carefully pushed the uterus back inside the cow.

Pete grimaced as Ginny put her arm into the cow all the way above her elbow. While she was holding the uterus in place, he watched as the cow decided it was time to urinate. Pete jumped back to keep urine from splashing on his shoes when it hit the ground and watched urine drip down Ginny's waterproof gown and shoe covers.

"Good reflexes!" Ginny said to Pete. She giggled. "You never know what's going to happen."

When the urine flow stopped, Ginny removed her arm and waited. A few minutes later, she saw a bulge that suggested the uterus was going to prolapse again. Reaching into her tool kit, Ginny retrieved suture material. After making sure everything was once again in place, Ginny stitched the opening just enough there could not be another prolapse.

After taking care of the cow, Brady let it out of the chute. As soon as the cow was free, the calf, which had been crying for its mother, became quiet and began to nurse.

"That's a good-looking calf, Tom," Ginny said after she checked it. "Hope you were wanting another bull."

"Nah. He'll be a steer I take to market," Tom said, "that is if there is a market." Tom paused, looked down at his well worn boots then back up at Ginny. "What do I owe you, Doc?"

"Well, Tom," Ginny said thoughtfully, "under the circumstances, can I delay payment? Then if you find that you are going to butcher that steer yourself, you can pay me in beef. How does that sound?"

"That sounds real good, Doc," Tom said. "Thank you. I won't forget."

"I know you won't, Tom," Ginny said, laughing. "But also, know this, I won't let you forget. I know you grow some of the best beef in three counties. My mama didn't raise a foolish girl."

"No, she didn't," Tom replied. "Your mama was a good one. We still miss her around here."

"I know, Tom. I do, too. Every day," Ginny said with a sad smile as she packed up her supplies. "You have a good night's sleep. Call me if there are any complications, but I'll be back in a few days to remove those sutures."

"I will. Thanks again, Doc," Tom said.

"You're very welcome, Tom," Ginny said warmly. "Glad I could help."

Pete helped Ginny replace her equipment inside the trailer. Ginny pulled out a plastic sheet and placed it on the passenger's seat.

"You can drive home," she said as she sat on the plastic.

"Glad to," Pete said as he walked around to the driver's side of the truck. He started the engine then looked at Ginny. "You're remarkable, do you know that?"

"Why, because I fixed a cow's butt?" Ginny said with a wave of her hand in the air. "That's nothing. Easy peasy."

"Not just that," Pete said. "You knew Tom Sutton couldn't pay, and you gave him a way to save his pride."

"Figured that out, did you?" Ginny asked as Pete pulled out of the Sutton's driveway and back onto the paved road. "I make enough on the horse business and those supplements that I can afford some pro bono work, especially now. With what's happening, who knows how long the money will be worth anything. Besides, I wasn't lying. He does grow the best beef in three counties. If he gives us a slab of beef for steaks, we will be eating very well, my friend."

The house was dark and quiet when they returned. Ginny got out, gathered the soiled plastic equipment and started toward the house. She looked up at the sky as she walked and wondered how everything could look so normal when it felt like the world was falling apart.

"I'll clean and restock tomorrow," she said with a sigh as they walked onto the back porch. "Let's just go to bed. I'm tired with a capital T."

"I'm sure you are," Pete said. "We were there almost four hours."

When they entered the mudroom, Brad came out of the office.

"Did you save another bovine life?" he asked.

Ginny giggled, "Yes."

"Did she pee on you?" he asked.

Ginny laughed out loud, "Yes. At least there was no poop. Pee is easier to clean off the tissue than manure."

Brad laughed. "I can only imagine. So, how is Tom paying you this time?"

"It was a little bull," Ginny said with a smile. "Tom wants to make it a steer and take it to market. If there's no market because of all this, he's going to pay me in steak!"

"That's better than cash! His beef is marvelous," Brad said.

"I know!" Ginny exclaimed.

Pete stood back watching Ginny and Brad. They had an easy friendship beyond being siblings. It was the type that came from several years of working together. He had never envied that before, but that just might be what he was feeling. The envy of family.

"Sis, go shower. You smell bad," Brad said holding his nose.

"Oh, you. Go to bed." Ginny tried to kiss him good night, but Brad intentionally squealed like a girl and ran. Ginny laughed harder.

Pete was grinning when Ginny turned on him.

"What?" she asked. "You think it's funny? You think I smell bad, too?"

Suddenly she was running toward him with her arms outstretched. A look of horror crossed Pete's face and he turned to run. Ginny collapsed in the floor laughing.

"Pete! The look on your face!" she squealed. "That was priceless!"

Ginny got up. She was laughing so hard tears were running down her face, and she was holding her stomach.

"That was so fun," Ginny said, trying to catch her breath. "I love it when I scare grown men."

Still giggling, Ginny went into the mudroom bathroom and showered for the second time that day. So much for Mark's orders of fewer showers.

Ginny came out of the bathroom with her hair wrapped in a towel and wearing sleep shorts and a t-shirt. Pete was sitting at the kitchen island drinking a glass of iced water.

"Why are you still awake?" she asked.

Pete looked at her and patted the stool beside him. "Have a seat."

"Is something wrong?" she asked.

"No," he answered.

Ginny sat on the stool with a worried look on her face. "What is it?"

"Ginny," Pete said softly as he faced her and leaned toward her ear, "the next time you come at me for a good night kiss, make sure you aren't covered in cow piss. Then, I will gladly oblige you." Pete stood from the stool and winked at her with a small grin tugging at his lips.

"Good night, Doc."

Ginny watched Pete go to his room with her mouth open in shock. What did he mean by that? She was just playing. Was he playing or was he serious? How was she supposed to know when he just walked out of the room? Thanks to growing up with three brothers, who did not hesitate to interfere with her choice of dates, and a very demanding program in college, she had zero experience with flirting. Now, she had a very handsome man say that to her.

Oh, great, she thought, *how am I supposed to get any sleep after that comment?* That was when she remembered that Holly would be asleep in her bedroom by now. She couldn't even go to her own bathroom and dry her hair. She didn't begrudge Holly her room. After all, Holly would be her sister-in-law. But tonight, she was tired, stressed, and bewildered by the events of the day and Pete's comment.

Looking at the clock on the microwave, Ginny saw that it was almost one in the morning. No wonder she was tired. Suddenly, it all crashed in on her. The number of people she was responsible for in her house, a country that was at war or at least heading that way, safety, responding to the demands of her job which had not stopped like others' jobs had, and now trying to determine what Pete meant.

Ginny put her hands on the island; her heart was beating fast, and she couldn't get her breath. *Slow your breathing. It's just anxiety. Nothing is wrong. Breathe slowly.* She was getting control of her emotions when she felt a hand on her shoulder.

"Ginny? What's wrong?" Pete asked. "Did I upset you?"

Ginny shook her head no and clenched her eyes shut. Still trying to control her breathing and stop the flow of tears that had started, she couldn't speak.

"Can you walk?" he asked.

Ginny nodded, and Pete took her hand.

"Come with me," he said and led her to the more formal parlor which was across from his room. He sat on the couch beside her and took her hand. "Are you having an anxiety attack?"

"I think so," she sputtered.

"I'm not surprised," he said. "You have all these people in your house, and you feel responsible, don't you."

Ginny nodded.

"Aw, Doc. I understand." He put his arms around her and whispered, "Feel my shoulder?"

Ginny nodded.

"It's pretty strong," he said, flexing his muscles to make a point. "Want to lean on it? You don't have to feel like you're handling everything alone. That's why Mark made so many assignments, so you wouldn't have to think about everything. He cares about you. That's why he wanted to take as much of the burden from you as he could. We all recognize that you and Brad still have your jobs to do. The rest of us will pick up the other things."

With her head on his shoulder, Pete rubbed Ginny's back until she began to breathe easier. Her breathing became soft and steady. Ginny's clenched hand softened in his, and he realized she had fallen asleep. He gently eased Ginny onto the couch and covered her with a quilt that looked handmade and had been draped over the back of the couch. He stayed there for a few minutes making sure she was still asleep before going to his own room to get some rest.

CHAPTER 16

APRIL 12

Pete yawned as he walked into the kitchen, heading to the coffee pot. It was well after 1:00 am when he got to bed the night before. Taking a sip of the strong black coffee, he looked around the room. Brad, Mark, and Garrett were huddled at the dining room table talking softly. He went over to the group.

"What's going on?" he asked.

"Ginny slept on the couch in the living room last night," Mark said. "She's still there. Know anything about that?"

Pete tried to decide if he needed to be angry with Ginny's brothers for their complete ignorance of their sister's feelings or laugh at their obvious confusion. He decided on neither. Instead, he turned and pointed to the front door.

"Step into my office," he said quietly, gesturing to the front porch.

Holly quietly watched the men leave the room. Barbara and Ceely came into the kitchen as the men were walking out the front door. Barbara walked to the screen door, looked out on the porch, and came back into the kitchen.

"What's going on out there?" she asked Holly. "Why does it look like the Reed brothers are ganging up on Pete?"

"I'm not sure," Holly replied. "I think it's more like Pete scolding them. Ginny slept in the parlor last night."

"The poor girl is exhausted," Barbara said. "I went to bed at eleven and they were still out with that cow."

"Maybe Pete's taking them to task," Ceely said as she looked at the morning's menu, "and maybe he should. I've always thought they take her for granted. They treat her house like it's still their parents' and they're still kids."

"That's the way of siblings, sometimes," Barbara said, taking eggs from the refrigerator. "We'll have to be more supportive to Ginny. Even though the place is organized like an army platoon, I'm sure she still feels responsible."

Ginny's brothers followed Pete to the porch and sat in the wicker chairs.

"Last night, Brad was the only one up when I brought Ginny home," Pete said. "She was tired and covered in cow piss. I was sitting at the island drinking a glass of water when she came out of the bathroom after showering. She sat beside me, and we talked for just a minute. I went to my room to go to bed. It was about one o'clock. I came out to go to the bathroom to finish getting ready for bed, and she was still at the kitchen island. She was struggling to catch her breath and was having an anxiety attack."

"Think about it," Pete said. "She was up before anyone yesterday to make breakfast. She heard about the attacks like we all did, delivered a foal, helped organize this group of people, helped with dinner, then just when she thought she could rest, she got called to help a neighbor with a cow in distress. She was exhausted when the full burden of feeling responsible for so many people in her home hit her like a wrecking ball.

"I couldn't just let her sit there in a panic. I took her into the parlor, let her cry on my shoulder, and rubbed her back until she started breathing normally. Then I realized she had fallen asleep. I didn't try to move her. I just covered her up and let her sleep."

Pete continued, "But here is my question to you. How can one woman have three brothers who don't even notice she's walking on the edge of panic? Mark, I know you did a great job organizing this group to take the burden off Ginny, but it doesn't stop her from feeling responsible. She works hard trying to make this a home for the rest of us, but she still has a full-time job like Brad does. How can we expect her to do the same amount of work around here as everyone else when she has a job to do? How do we help her?"

Mark, Brad and Garrett looked at each other then back at Pete.

"I thought we had," Garrett said. "Mark arranged the whole place around her."

"Ginny always works like this," Brad said. "This is nothing new, Pete. This is her way. She takes care of everyone."

"Who takes care of Ginny?" Pete asked.

The three men looked at Pete in confusion.

"I did," Mark said. "I organized everyone so she wouldn't have the burden of telling people what to do."

Pete realized he was never going to convince his friends that Ginny needed more than an organizational chart.

"Okay. I guess that's settled then. Maybe we should go eat breakfast." Pete stood and walked back into the house.

Mark, Brad and Garrett looked at each other with stunned confusion.

"What was that about?" Brad asked.

Mark looked thoughtful, "It sounds to me like Pete may be developing feelings for Ginny. He was very protective of her. He may not even realize that's what's happening." He grinned. "This might be fun to watch."

"Do we help it along?" asked Garrett.

"Not yet," Mark said. "Let's pay more attention to Ginny and how she acts around him. Then we can decide if we should throw them together more."

"In all honesty," Mark said, looking at his brothers, "Pete would make a great husband. He's one of the best men I have ever known or worked with. I would trust him with Ginny's life. I say we encourage it, carefully."

Brad and Garrett agreed. Smiling, the men walked into the house to eat breakfast.

While Brad, Mark, Garrett and Pete talked on the porch, Ginny woke up and went upstairs to her room. She needed to change clothes and comb her hair. Thinking about last night, she decided she needed to thank Pete for calming her down and not waking her when she fell asleep.

At eight o'clock, Brad knocked on Ginny's door.

"Ginny, are you in here?" he called out.

When she didn't answer, he opened the door and saw Ginny coming out of her bathroom. She was dressed and pulling her hair back.

"I'm up and ready," she answered. "When are we going to Elkin?"

"As soon as you eat," he said. "Everyone is downstairs having breakfast."

Ginny followed Brad down the stairs and helped herself to an egg burrito.

Ginny took a bite of the burrito and exclaimed, "This is delicious! Who made these?"

Everyone pointed to Erica.

"Erica, make a list of the ingredients," Ginny said. "I'm buying a case of each in Elkin. Can we have these at least once a week?"

Erica smiled and said, "Sure, as long as we have flour, eggs, and the spices. I'll make the list for you."

The plan was for Brad to drive his truck, and Alex to drive his SUV. The morning was cool which made it easy to hide a pistol under their layers of shirts and jackets. Rifles and shotguns were placed in the vehicles.

"This is day three," Pete told the group as they gathered in the backyard. "People will not be as nice today as they have been the last two. Stay alert."

"At each store, Alex will stay with the vehicles," Mark said. "Brad and I will take one list. Ginny and Pete will take the other. One shops while the other one guards the cart and the shopper. Understood?"

Everyone said, "Yes."

"All right then," Mark said. "Let's get this done and get back."

The first stop was the discount store on the edge of town. The parking lot was already full, and the store had been open only thirty minutes. Brad and Alex drove through the parking lot until they found spaces where they could park beside each other. Alex stood between the vehicles while the others went inside.

Ginny and Pete took a cart and went to the toiletry section. Most shelves were empty, and there were no employees restocking the items. Ginny found a few bottles of shampoo and some toothpaste on the floor under the shelves or behind unwanted merchandise. She was able to only get a few of the personal items she needed. As they were passing through the toy section on the way to the camping area Ginny found a display of batteries. She took two packs of every size. In the camping area she found insect repellent, two sleeping bags, fire starters, charcoal, and emergency candles. On impulse, Ginny went to the children's department and got underwear, socks and pajamas in every size available. Then in the shoe department she did the same, athletic shoes and boots in every size she could find.

Pete and Ginny were finished before their thirty-minute limit was up and got into the checkout line. Mark and Brad came up later and got in the same line. Ginny and Pete bought their items and waited inside the store for Mark and Brad. Once they finished purchasing everything, the four walked their carts to the SUV. Quickly placing everything in the back, they got in and drove away.

"That was tense," Ginny said. "I had no idea it was like this."

"It'll get worse," Pete said. "It didn't look like a full truck had been there to resupply the store. Or if it has, it wasn't enough. Everyone is panic buying, including us."

A chain pharmacy was the next stop. The same procedure was followed. Ginny found a few more toiletry items here, but she wasn't surprised. The prices were slightly higher than the discount store. Ginny found a few large storage bins and got those so they could put things in the bed of the pickup.

The group went to every discount store and pharmacy in Elkin. Their last stop was the grocery store that had higher prices but a larger selection of food. In fact, their prices were twice as high as the prices in other stores. There, Ginny found the spices she needed for Erica's burritos. She also put as many flour and corn tortillas that she could find in the cart. This store still had some fresh fruits and vegetables left. Ginny got two or three of everything along with bacon, sausage, dairy products and ice cream. The others got baking staples and canned fruits and vegetables.

The two groups checked out at the same time. As they were going out the door a group of six men stood in the parking lot watching them push the carts to the vehicles. They formed a line and started to slowly approach Brad's truck.

"Three o'clock," Mark said without turning around.

"See them," answered Pete. "Take the carts between the vehicles."

Alex stood just to the left of his driver's seat, watching the men from across the hood of the SUV. He casually laid his shotgun on the hood's surface. Pete stood in the space between the vehicles, watching the men, his hand resting on his pistol. Mark rested his rifle on the side of the truck bed. The guns were in a nonthreatening position but were there to make sure the men knew they were armed.

The men had gotten to within a row of parking places near the vehicles. They stopped when they saw the guns, put their hands in the air and backed away.

Between the truck and SUV, Ginny and Brad quickly loaded the supplies.

"Ginny, get in the SUV on your side," Pete said when the carts were empty. "Just push the stuff out of the way." Ginny did as she was instructed.

Alex was already behind the wheel when Pete got into the passenger's seat. Mark pushed the carts out of the way then got into the passenger's seat of Brad's truck, and Brad climbed in behind the wheel. Together, they left the parking lot and headed home. Brad was in the lead and decided to leave town the opposite way from their house then backtrack. When they were sure they weren't being followed, he turned and drove back to the farm. The ride back was quiet. No one spoke. They were all processing the changes that were taking place in their world that was becoming difficult to recognize.

When they got back to the farm, Pete walked around the back of the SUV to Ginny who was climbing out of the back seat.

"Are you okay?" he asked her.

"Yes, I'm fine," she said. "I find this whole situation needless, and it should have been avoided. But I'm not fearful. I feel like we're in good shape on the farm to survive through whatever's happening. I was just surprised by the level of tension you could actually feel in those stores. People are scared."

"Yeah, I noticed it too," Pete said, nodding. "Hopefully things won't get worse."

Ginny nodded and followed Pete to the back of the SUV where the others were already unloading supplies.

When Ginny walked into the kitchen, Erica took the bags from her and asked, "How was it?"

"Not bad, but it was very tense. People are afraid," Ginny said as she started removing items from the bags. "At the last grocery store a group of men watched the whole time we were unloading and even started to approach us. Alex, Mark and Pete knew exactly what to do. That gives me a lot of reassurance if things don't get better soon."

"I know," Erica replied. "They're well trained, but I don't think we'll have too many problems out in the country like this."

Barbara came into the room with her clipboard and ink pen.

"Oh fun!" she said. "More goodies to inventory."

"We've created an organizational monster!" Ceely exclaimed. All the women were laughing when the men brought the last of the supplies into the kitchen.

"What's so funny?" Mark asked.

Ceely patted him on the cheek and said, "It's a girl thing, honey. Don't worry your pretty little head over it." The women laughed harder.

"You think my head is pretty, huh," Mark said, grinning and moving his eyebrows up and down. "I think I like that." Everyone laughed when Mark made his wife blush by kissing her in front of the group.

CHAPTER 17

APRIL 12

Later that afternoon, Pete and Alex had finished walking the perimeter of the farm and were sitting on the front porch discussing security issues with Mark and Robert. Ginny walked out and sat down in one of the empty chairs to listen. She observed the men as they talked about problems and possible solutions. Each one had his own specific strengths which he brought to the discussion. After about thirty minutes, they had a plan and a timetable to accomplish it.

"What do you think, Ginny?" Mark asked.

"I think you're all marvelous, and I thank God you're all here. I don't know what Brad and I would have done without you. What can I do to help?" she asked.

"We'll let you decide when to take down the mailbox," Mark said. "We'll sow grass seed across the driveway and transplant a few small trees. Right now, I'm glad Mom and Dad never paved it."

"I'll check the mail on the way to the Johnson's. Can you spare Pete?" she asked. "I want to check on the mare and filly, and Aaron wants to discuss security with Pete."

"I can go with you," Pete said as he stood. "We're done here."

"Thanks. Let me get my truck keys," Ginny said. Pete opened the door for her, and the two walked back into the house.

Mark, Brad, and Garrett looked at each other and smiled.

"What?" asked Alex. "Am I missing something?"

"We think Pete is developing an interest in Ginny," Mark said.

"That's understandable," Robert said. "They're the only single adults here."

"I'd believe it," Alex added. "He was interested in her at the airport before we knew all this was happening. I just hadn't thought any more about it. They're both great. I think it would work."

"We're not pushing anything," Garrett said. "We're just watching, but they can't know that, or it would spoil everything. The last thing we want is for any awkwardness to develop in tight quarters like this. That would be bad for the whole household. So, no smiles, snickers, knowing looks, no nothin'. Agreed?"

They all agreed.

"Good," Mark said. "Now, we have work to do."

Ginny handed Pete her truck keys.

"Would you drive?" she asked. "I want to check the mail and my records before we get to the Johnson's."

"Sure," Pete said and climbed into the driver's seat.

At the end of the driveway, Ginny discovered that the mail had run.

"I guess we wait another day before taking up the mailbox," she said. "Take a right and the next drive on the right. It's close, only a few yards away."

Pete nodded, and a few minutes later they were pulling into the Johnson's drive.

"Their house is definitely very close to the road," he said. Pete observed the two story farmhouse as they passed it, and he parked behind it.

Aaron and Donna came out the back door.

"Hey, Ginny," Aaron said. "Good to see you. Did you come to check on Star?"

"I did. Aaron, this is Pete Flinn," Ginny said as she introduced Pete to the Johnsons. "He's an army buddy of Mark's who is staying with us for now. Pete is from Chicago and is the security expert I told you about."

"Nice to meet ya, Pete," Aaron said as he shook Pete's hand. "I was sorry to hear about Chicago. Did your place there get hit?"

"I don't know yet," Pete answered. "What little information we've found said that the bombs were randomly placed all over the city. I live on the west side, almost to Aurora. I may be okay. I'll just have to wait and see. Ginny said you wanted to talk about your farm."

"Yeah, I do. Want to take a look?" Aaron asked as he led Pete to his office in the barn where he had aerial pictures of the farm. "I wanted to talk away from Donna. She's getting nervous about everything. I love her, but she's a worrier."

"I understand." Pete said as he began looking at the pictures. He had Aaron show him the borders of his farm and asked questions about the farm to the west. Aaron told him it was owned by the Smith family and that he rented the entire farm for its pastures and cropland. Seeing that Aaron's land, both owned and rented, was bordered on three sides by the highway, Pete began a preliminary plan which he discussed with Aaron.

Outside the barn, Ginny said, "Donna, would you like to come with me to see Star? I haven't talked with you in ages."

Donna smiled as she walked with Ginny to the small pasture behind the barn. Her petite frame seemed dwarfed by the larger mare. The auburn strands of her brown hair were highlighted in the afternoon sun, and her dark eyes shined with humor as she watched the foal trying to nurse its mother.

Ginny checked the animals and declared them healthy.

"I imagine Bonnie hasn't left them for very long at a time," Ginny said as she finished her examination.

"You're right about that," Donna said, laughing. "I have to force her to come into the house to finish her schoolwork and eat."

"I heard the kids are on remote learning right now," Ginny said as the two women walked back to the house. "How's that going?"

"Not bad," Donna answered. "My kids know they have to keep up. We stay on them about that. I imagine there are other homes that are not as compliant or have no computers, and the kids are just watching TV. I would think the teachers are frustrated over this. At least we have a farm and property so our kids can get outside. I would be going crazy if my kids had to stay inside all the time." She sighed, "I'll be so glad when all of this is over."

"Me too, Donna," Ginny said.

The two women were standing in the barnyard when they heard the screen door on the back porch slam shut. They looked up to see Bonnie leaving the house.

"Miss Ginny!" Bonnie called, running toward the barn. "How are Star and Sunshine?"

"You named her!" Ginny exclaimed. "I like that name. Sunshine is fine and healthy, and so is Star. You take good care of your animals, Bonnie. I'm proud of you."

Bonnie smiled at the compliment and walked into the pasture to pet the foal.

"She's a good girl, Donna," Ginny said. "I know you're proud of your children."

"Yes. I am," Donna said with a smile. "I'm worried about my sister, though. She's divorced, and it's just her and her daughter who's Bonnie's age. Phone calls are impossible. Even texting is hard."

"Where do they live?" Ginny asked.

"Just north of Charlotte," Donna said. "She teaches in Huntersville."

"Have you heard from her?" Ginny asked.

"Not today," Donna said. "She's supposed to come here, but I don't know her progress."

"Well, I hope she appears on your doorstep. I know you'll feel better," Ginny said reassuringly.

Pete and Aaron had come out of the barn, and the four were walking toward Ginny's truck when an SUV entered the driveway and came to the back of the house. The door opened and a woman slightly older than Donna got out. Donna ran to the car and hugged the woman.

"That's her sister, Grace," Aaron said. "Donna's been worried about her. The girl is our niece, Hannah. I'm glad they made it. I've been a little concerned myself."

Donna brought the woman and her daughter to meet Ginny and Pete.

"Ginny, Pete, this is my sister, Grace and her daughter, Hannah," Donna said.

"It's nice to meet you both," Ginny said as she shook Grace's hand. "I'm glad you made it here."

"Glad to meet you," Pete said. "May I ask, how are things around Charlotte?"

"Terrible," Grace said. "The bombs went off just as school was starting, which was awful. It was rush hour." Grace shook her head, "So many people injured or killed. The TV stations in Charlotte are off the air, except for sporadic coverage from remote crews who were not at the station when the bombs went off. My neighbor has a drone, and he showed us pictures." Grace shook her head.

"The bridges on I-277 were destroyed. The Bank of America Building is gutted from fire, and most of the buildings around it are in rubble. The stadium is ruined, but the worst part is the damage to the residential areas. I only hope the residents were gone, heading to school or work.

"We could hear the explosions all the way in Huntersville. Schools were immediately closed. I took Hannah with me, and we went to the bank for cash and to our large grocery store to get medications, food, and other supplies. The traffic and crowds at the stores were so heavy that the errands took us all day. We spent yesterday packing.

"We left this morning at 6:00, and it still took nine hours to get here. Traffic is bumper to bumper and slow everywhere but this side of Elkin. The roads are clogged with people leaving Charlotte. Everyone is scared there will be more bombs. People started panic buying which has emptied the stores of groceries and supplies. People are leaving and hoping to find food and safety.

"There are two gangs in the area that I know about. We heard they have become rivals and anyone in their way is just killed and tossed to the side. Unfortunately, a lot of the police force were killed in the bombs. People in Charlotte are at the mercy of the gangs right now. I've never seen anything like this. It's like a horror movie or another country, not ours.

"When I saw how crowded I-77 was, I didn't even try to get on it. We took back roads all the way up. That's what has taken so long. We were lucky enough to find a gas station open on a rural road, or we might be stranded along the way, too.

"Where will all those people go?" Ginny asked.

"We traveled over a bridge that crossed the interstate north of Statesville," Grace said. "The interstate was still bumper to bumper, and there were cars that had pulled over to the side. I imagine they ran out of gas."

Grace looked at Donna and Aaron, "Thank you so much for letting us come here."

"Grace, we would have been upset and worried if you hadn't come," Aaron said, reassuring her. "Family sticks together." Grace smiled back at him.

"Pete and I need to be getting back," Ginny said, placing her hand on Aaron's arm. She looked at his relatives, "Grace, it's been nice to meet you."

When Pete and Ginny were back in the truck, Ginny said, "I want to check the mailbox at the clinic. Take a right then the next road to the right. Now tell me what you and Aaron discussed."

"He realizes they are sitting ducks for problems," Pete said, "especially if refugees start to come this way, or someone like those Larkin boys want to make trouble. He's especially worried for his kids, and now he has another teenage girl to think about. Did you know he has a barn on the north side of the farm next to your property and that it has a small apartment above it instead of a full loft?"

"I knew about the barn, but I didn't know it had an apartment," Ginny said.

"If the worst happened and they had to leave the house, that would be a good place for them to go." Pete said as he turned right at the stop sign. "It's isolated and can't be seen from the road. Ginny, Aaron said he went into Elkin earlier this afternoon. He went to the parking lot at the big box store. The Larkin boys and their friends were there, and they were harassing people as they came out of the store, especially any women. He said Elkin's like a ghost town now. No one is on the streets, and the police are patrolling the town. He hasn't heard of any crime, but that may not be far away if things don't get better nationally. He went to that upscale grocery store that we went to yesterday. It's almost empty. The manager said they had a delivery truck this morning, but what they put on the shelves was gone in under thirty minutes, and the prices had doubled again."

Pete made a right turn into the parking lot of the clinic. Ginny got the mail and brought it back to the truck.

"I want to check inside. I'll be right back," she said. She unlocked the door, entered the clinic and checked every room and the storeroom one more time. Ginny came back to the truck with a bag of supplies.

"I found these," she said. "They were in the reception area I forgot to check the other night. Also, the power's out. No lights came on when I flipped the switches. I checked the breaker box. It was fine; no breakers had been tripped. I guess we'd better get back to the farm and see if the power is out there, too. Take a right, and we'll make a circle back to the house. I want to see what things look like on this part of the road."

Pete left the parking lot and drove the truck slowly back to the house, taking care to memorize the land on both sides of the road. The bright sunshine of the late afternoon made it easy to see everything. Ginny showed him where her farm ended and the Thompson farm started. She told him the Thompsons were retired and that Brad had bought their farm. After turning right at the next road, Ginny showed him where the Sutton farm began and ended, which was where hers began.

"You have road frontage on two sides of your farm?" Pete asked.

"Just a little," she said. "The clinic is on the point where our farm reaches the road. To the right is the Thompson farm, and to the left is the Smith farm which is behind the Johnson's. Aaron Johnson rents the Smith farm, but you already know that. I noticed the grass growing up around the clinic and behind it. The trail I use to drive from the house to the clinic is starting to look overgrown. I don't want to cut it. If someone tries to break into the clinic, it will probably be at night, and they won't notice a path of any sort."

"It's definitely a nice commute," Pete said. "Letting the grass grow up around it is wise." He turned right and drove through the woods to the farm. He parked the truck behind the equipment shed, and the two walked back to the house, ready for dinner.

CHAPTER 18

APRIL 12

When Pete and Ginny walked into the house, they were greeted with the aroma of beef stew. Barbara was mixing a large bowl of cole slaw, and Ceely was taking biscuits out of the oven. Leah was putting out napkins, silverware, bowls and plates on the kitchen island.

"You're just in time for dinner," Barbara said. "I wasn't sure we were going to finish it. The power went off, but your generator started. It ran for about fifteen minutes before power was restored. We didn't know you had that little backup system. That's quite nice!"

"Any word on why the power went out?" Pete asked.

"Adam, Brett, and Michael are checking on it. The three of them are looking at different news sites," Leah answered as she gently pushed the napkins safely away from the edge of the island.

"Don't you have a generator at the clinic?" Pete asked Ginny.

"I do," Ginny said, "but I disengaged it the other night. It's emergency only and not meant to do anything but keep computers on and the surgery lights and equipment running. It runs on propane, so I thought I would preserve what was in the tanks."

Ceely went to the basement stairs and called down to the girls who were playing with their dolls. Barbara went to the front porch to get the boys. Everyone came into the kitchen for dinner. The group had settled into a routine. Garrett said the blessing, and everyone lined up at the kitchen island for food. The girls went to the card table, the boys went to the breakfast nook, and the adults sat at the dining room table.

The girls finished eating and asked to be excused. Barbara took them back to the basement where they resumed their play. When she returned, Pete told the adults what he and Ginny had heard from Aaron and Grace.

"It sounds like Charlotte isn't a nice place to be right now," Alex said. "Can you get those news stations here?"

"Yes," Brad said, "but we usually watch the Winston station since it's closer to us than Charlotte. Maybe we should start checking all the websites."

Mark began to outline the plans for improved security around the farm. Brad and Ginny owned a few solar powered game cameras. He, Pete, and Alex were going to place those cameras in strategic locations, and they would be programmed to record continuously. Pictures would be sent to a computer that would be set up in the den. A schedule would be made so that the computer would always be monitored.

Ginny's phone rang, which startled everyone because they had been listening intently to Mark.

"This is Dr. Reed," she said and paused. "Has he been ridden today? Is he in the pasture? Do you have a barn stall that is not on concrete? Put him there until I get there." Pause. "Hopefully in an hour. Give him water, no food." Ginny ended the call. "I need to go. Sounds like laminitis."

"Where?" asked Mark.

Ginny rolled her eyes. "A new horse farm east of Elkin. They moved in last year, and I get at least one call a week out there. These people had never been around horses and suddenly decided they want a horse farm. They have no clue how to properly care for them. I spend more time teaching than treating."

"I'm coming with you," Pete said, standing, "especially if you are going through Elkin and over the interstate."

"Fine," Ginny said, already moving toward the stairs. "I'm changing into work clothes. Meet you at the truck in fifteen minutes."

A few minutes later, Ginny came down the stairs in skinny jeans and a long sleeve t-shirt with Reed Animal Clinic on the back. Stopping in the mud room, she put on a pair of knee-high rubber boots. Ginny found her medical records for the horse farm, checked her supplies, and got into the truck's driver seat. She watched Pete come around the equipment shed. He carried a pump action shotgun, and a rifle was slung over his shoulder.

"Expecting trouble?" Ginny asked, raising her eyebrows as she watched Pete put the guns on the back seat.

"Hope not," Pete replied as he climbed into the passenger seat. "But we're going through Elkin and then crossing I-77. Who knows what we'll encounter. My advice would be that after tonight you turn down any calls on the other side of the interstate."

"Why?" Ginny asked as she started the engine.

"Is there a hill before you get to the interstate?" Pete asked. "One that will allow you to stop and see the bridge?"

"Yes," Ginny replied.

"Good. Stop on the hill. I'll show you," he instructed.

"All right," Ginny said as she drove down the driveway.

Ginny drove the bypass around Elkin. So far, there had been no other traffic on the road. On the hill just before the interstate she pulled to the side of the road and turned off the engine.

"Watch the road," Pete said. He took a pair of binoculars that he had brought along and studied the bridge for almost a full minute. Then he handed the binoculars to Ginny.

"Look through these," he said. "Focus on the right side of the road just before the bridge. What do you see?"

"There are people in the ditch. Looks like two men," Ginny said, watching two men kneeling in the ditch with their heads below the level of the road. They were barely visible in the long shadows of the waning sunlight. A blue truck was parked in the shadows of the trees behind them.

"Now, look across the bridge," he instructed.

"There are more men along the side of the road. Why would men be hiding on the side of the road like that? Is it a trap?" Ginny asked incredulously. She had no experience with danger like this.

"Probably," Pete answered. A pickup truck drove past them toward the bridge. "Watch that truck and see what happens."

When the truck got close to the bridge, two men stepped out from the bushes and stopped it. One went to the window and talked to the driver. The other man stood watching, his shotgun visible. The driver backed up, turned around and drove back toward town. Seeing Ginny in her truck, he slowed and rolled down his window.

"Lady," he said, "don't go down there. If you try to cross that bridge without paying the toll they want, it will not go well."

"Thank you," Ginny answered. The man nodded and drove away.

"Ginny, we need to turn around and go home," Pete said emphatically.

"What about that poor horse?" she asked.

"You can call them and give them instructions over the phone," Pete said. "What just happened at the bridge is why I'm telling you to turn down calls from across the highway."

"I had no idea," she said. "Where are the police?"

"I don't know," Pete replied. "They may not be aware of what's happening yet. I'm surprised this has already started. I thought we had another day or two. Those are opportunists of the worst kind. The police may make them leave, but they'll just come right back."

"Thank you, Pete," she said, looking at him gratefully. "I understand what you're saying, and I'm so glad you're here. I would have driven right into that trap. I have narcotics in the back. I hate to think what they would've been willing to do to steal them."

"Want me to drive home?" Pete asked.

"No," Ginny answered, starting the engine back up. "I'm fine. I'd rather you be the lookout."

The ride back to the farm was quiet. Ginny was processing the changes that were taking place, and Pete kept his eyes on the road. He watched the road for trouble ahead of them and the side mirror to make sure they weren't being followed.

Ginny parked the truck in its usual spot behind the equipment shed. When they had both gotten out of the truck, Ginny impulsively hugged Pete.

"Thank you," she said. "I can't tell you how much I appreciate you and your knowledge. You may have saved my life, more than once if we count the last few days."

"I'm glad I was there," Pete said as he hugged her back and kissed the top of her head. "Now you know why I insisted on going with you."

"Yes. I understand," Ginny said as she released him. "I need to call the owners of that horse. They aren't going to like what I have to say." Ginny pulled her phone from her pocket and dialed the horse owner.

Pete left her and walked toward the house. It was almost dark, so he turned on the porch light as he went inside.

"That was fast," Mark said. He looked at Pete, "You didn't get there, did you. What happened?"

Pete told the group what was going on at the bridge across the interstate.

"I saw an old blue pickup in the trees on our side of the bridge," Pete told the group. "It was the same one I saw in town the other day. I believe their name was Larkin."

"Ugh!" Holly groaned. "Yes. They're hoodlums. I'm not surprised they're doing that. Where were the police?"

"That's what we were wondering," Pete said. "It could be the Larkins do that until they see law enforcement, and then they scatter. When the police leave, they return."

"At least they were on the other side of Elkin and not close to us," Mark said.

Ginny walked into the house.

"How did it go?" Pete asked.

"They weren't happy," she said. "They couldn't grasp the gravity of the situation in Elkin or the condition of their horse and how they had contributed to it. I gave them the number of a vet in Mt. Airy. He wouldn't have to cross the interstate to get to the farm. The owner was angry enough to say he would never call me again. I'm not sorry about that. I hate dealing with people who mistreat their animals out of sheer ignorance and pride."

Brad had been outside locking the buildings. He walked into the house just as Ginny was replacing her records in the office. Brad entered the room behind her.

"Hey, sis, did I see you hugging Pete?" Brad asked.

Ginny turned to Brad and said, "Yes. I was so grateful. Brad, he probably saved my life by keeping me out of a road trap. We never got to the horse farm."

Brad hugged Ginny, "I'm sorry that happened. I may have to hug Pete myself."

Ginny laughed. "Can I watch?"

Brad kissed the top of her head.

"Pete did that too, just like my brothers," she said. "See, nothing there. Stop worrying." Ginny left the room.

"I need to talk with him about that," Brad said softly to himself as he left the room. "He needs to go for the lips."

Brad walked back into the den just as Adam came in waving his phone in the air.

"Hey everybody," he announced, "turn on the TV. I think we retaliated against North Korea."

Robert turned the television to the Winston Salem station. The news was all about what had happened. During the night in Asia, the US had sent large attack drones under the radar to the North Korean border and fired missiles that hit most of the nuclear weapon silos in North Korea, rendering them unusable. While the US had not used nuclear missiles, when one of the silos was hit, the safety mechanisms malfunctioned and the nuclear warhead detonated.

Fortunately, for most of the people of North Korea, those explosions were in remote locations. No cities had been hit. The President was waiting to hear from the Secretary of Defense as to the full extent of the damage. It was reported that the ambassador from China was currently in contact with the President.

"I guess we wait and see what happens," Garrett said.

"I wonder if North Korea or China will retaliate," Alex said. "I guess we'll find out tomorrow. It seems both sides are making their strikes at night or early morning."

CHAPTER 19

APRIL 13

At dawn, Ginny dressed in jeans and a t-shirt and tiptoed out of the bedroom, leaving Holly sleeping. It was her turn to fix breakfast, so she started the first pots of coffee, still thankful for the extra coffee maker Mark had brought. Checking the menu notebook on the counter, she saw that eggs and pancakes were listed for today. No meat. Leah was already rationing the bacon and sausage that was left.

Pouring herself a cup of coffee, Ginny tiptoed out to the front porch. The morning was brisk but pleasant. The eastern pink sky was fading to blue as the sun rose above the horizon. Ginny said a morning prayer of thanks then closed her eyes and listened. All the sounds of the farm brought comfort. Birds singing, cows lowing softly in the pasture, chickens clucking to be let out of the coop, and the sound of Barf coming up the front steps for his morning pets. They all made Ginny smile with contentment, which was welcomed in the midst of the turmoil and uncertainty of the future.

Ginny heard a male voice say, "Good morning." She opened her eyes and smiled.

"Good morning, Pete. You're up early."

"That's my routine," he said as he sat down beside her. "I've always been an early riser. Even as a kid."

"Me too," Ginny said, reaching down to pet Barf. "I like the stillness and the sounds of early morning."

"Early morning is different here than in the Chicago suburbs," Pete observed as he looked out across the yard. "No traffic or sirens."

Ginny smiled. "I know. Nice isn't it." She watched Barf move to Pete for attention.

"Yes, it is," he said, absent-mindedly petting the dog. "If I lived here, I wouldn't want to leave either."

"What do you think today will bring?" Ginny asked. "Since all this started it seems all we have had are surprises. No routine."

"Who knows," Pete said. "This is day four. I guess things will depend on whether North Korea or China decide to slap our hands or try to give us a knockout punch. Plus, we still don't have a handle on exactly who set off the bombs or if there are any more surprises coming from them."

"Let's go turn on the television," Ginny said, standing. "I need to prep breakfast."

The two walked back into the house. Barf followed them, hoping for food. Ginny went to the mudroom to feed the dog then started gathering eggs and milk from the refrigerator. Pete went to the den and turned the TV to the Winston Salem channel.

The news showed pictures of the devastation in the cities from the bombs. There were videos of people rioting and looting in the large cities. They also showed pictures from across the nation of people who were stranded along the interstates in their cars or tents where they ran out of gas. Most had been trying to leave the cities due to terrorist bombs, crime and the lack of supplies. The Red Cross and local municipalities were trying to help as much as they could, but it was turning into a humanitarian crisis.

"That's awful," sounded from the back of the den.

When Pete heard the comment, he turned to see Ceely and Mark standing behind him, watching the television.

"Those poor people," Ceely said. "Mark, I am so glad you said we had to leave when we did. That could be us."

"Or us," Barbara said as she walked into the den to see the television. "We left later than you did."

"Have they said anything more about North Korea?" Alex asked, walking up with a mug of coffee in his hand.

"Not yet, unless it was reported before I turned the television on," Pete replied.

At 8:00, Ginny announced that breakfast was ready just as the kids ran up the stairs from the basement. The television was turned off, Garrett said the blessing, and everyone lined up at the kitchen island for food.

"What's on schedule for today?" Ginny asked as she settled into her seat at the dining room table.

"I'm on track to finish the outhouse," Robert reported. "All we will need are magazines and toilet paper," he said teasingly. "That and lime. Brad has a pallet of lime in the fertilizer shed. I'll put a small cup with one bag. When you use the toilet, toss a cup of lime in to speed up decomposition and keep odors down." Robert made a comical gesture using his empty coffee cup. "Ladies, it will also have a toilet seat for your sitting comfort."

"Our comfort? Don't you mean your comfort while you read your magazines?" Leah asked, grinning slyly at Robert. Everyone at the table laughed.

"Or that," Robert said smiling. He turned to Ginny, "We need to discuss where you want the outdoor shower. We'll start that tomorrow." Ginny nodded in agreement.

"Alex and I are going to mount the game cameras in the trees to monitor the road and driveway," Pete said.

"I'm going to plant corn," Brad said. "I hope there's a market this fall, but if not, we can always use it for chicken feed. I'm going to plant several rows of sweet corn for us. I'm going to increase the size of the garden, too. Let some of the lettuce, onions, cabbage, green peas and asparagus go to seed. We'll need to harvest the seeds if we want a garden next year."

"I'm going to do laundry today," Ginny said. "If anyone has dark clothes they need to wash, put them in the laundry room. All of my work clothes are filthy."

"I will attest to that statement," Pete said. "Does cow piss stain?"

Ginny rolled her eyes at him, and the others laughed. As if on cue, Ginny's phone rang.

"This is Dr. Reed." Ginny listened then said, "You're probably right. Is she still standing? I'll be there as soon as I can." Ginny ended the call.

"Another foal," she said, looking at Pete. "This one is just north of here about two miles. I don't think you need to come this time."

"She's right, Pete," Mark said. "I know that farm. It won't take her five minutes to get there. Your time is better spent placing the game cameras."

"If you say so," Pete answered. "I have to trust you. I don't know the area."

Ginny collected her medical records and supplies then left for the horse farm. Everyone else gathered supplies, and soon the house was quiet as people left to work.

Mark took his cellphone to the front porch and made some calls. After cleaning the kitchen, Ceely joined him.

"What's up?" she asked.

"I was just trying to find out what I could about the international situation," Mark answered. "Everyone seems to be holding their breath and hoping diplomacy works. The military is on high alert. All nonmilitary Americans are being evacuated from South Korea, southeast Asia, and the south Pacific. Military personnel from various US bases around the world are being ordered back to the United States.

"I'm afraid that with the US preoccupied, other countries will take the opportunity to do things they wouldn't normally do. We can't currently help our allies. We're too busy taking care of our own, which is fine with me. The NATO countries have not exactly jumped on the bandwagon to help us out."

"Ceely," he said, "I'm worried about your brother, Mike. He and Heather live in Greensboro, and they have a toddler. I'd like to know they're safe, and the only way to ensure that is to invite them here."

"But where would they stay?" Ceely asked. "The house is completely full. Plus, I don't want to add any more stress onto Ginny."

"You know we've talked about getting a camper," Mark said. "How do you feel about buying a small one today? The camper dealer in Sparta has a few in stock. It's just up the mountain, and we wouldn't have to cross a major four lane road. Mom and Dad built two RV sites out back, so it would be a good place to put one. Mike and his family could stay there."

"I love the idea," she said with no hesitation. "I brought the checkbook for the savings account. Let's get something we like. Then we can use it for family vacations when this is all over."

"I'll tell Garrett," Mark said as he stood. "Get ready and grab a jacket. It'll be cooler on the mountain than here. I'll call Mike when we get back."

An hour later, Mark and Ceely were negotiating the price of a travel trailer and six tanks of propane. Two hours later, the trailer was hitched to the back of their SUV and the two were driving it back down the mountain.

Chapter 20

April 13

Ginny stood next to her work truck, retrieving her bag of dirty supplies when Mark drove the trailer into the yard and toward the RV sites. Ginny walked up to the camper.

"Nice trailer, Mark. What brought this on?" she asked, adjusting her ball cap to block the late morning sun as she inspected the new addition to the farm.

"There are two sites here," he said. "I want to put this on one. I called Ceely's brother, Mike. He and Heather left Greensboro because it was getting unsafe. They're currently camping in tents at Stone Mountain. I told them to come here. They were relieved to have somewhere to go and should be here later this afternoon.

Ginny looked at her brother. She frowned, and Mark could see the worry in her face. He knew she was concerned about the number of people coming to the farm and how to fit everyone in comfortably and safely.

"Ginny," Mark said with mild firmness, "it's Ceely's brother and his family. They're part of our family, and we were worried about them. Plus, they have a two-year-old son."

"I know," Ginny said with a resigned sigh. "It's okay. I just worry about everyone being comfortable and about the food situation." Suddenly, Ginny's quiet resignation turned to frustration. She gave Mark a direct, pointed look.

"You know what, Mark," she said firmly and raising her hand in frustration, "it's not okay. Not one person has addressed the cost that all these people are adding to my utility bills. Did you think about that?" Ginny felt her anger growing with every word. "Every person outside our immediate family, except Holly, has been arbitrarily added by you. You never discussed even one with me. At least Brad asked me before he invited Holly. You would never have done that to Mom and Dad, but this is *my* house and *my* farm, now. You cannot add any more people without consulting me first, is that clear? Also, I expect you to have everyone contribute to the astronomical power bills that will start arriving."

Mark stood still. He was shocked. He had never seen this adult, assertive side of his sister before. He still remembered her as the quiet, easy going sister from when their parents were alive. He never even questioned her buying his part of the farm because it had been to his advantage.

"You're right," he said calmly. "From now on, no more decisions without collaboration. Hand me the utility bills when they come. I'll collect the money. Let's not worry until we have to."

"Good," Ginny said, "and you're sounding like Garrett. Don't worry until it's necessary."

Mark walked back to the camper, which was parked on the level site next to the equipment shed. His mind was reeling from the paradigm shift taking place where Ginny was concerned. He needed to process this change, so he started the task of leveling the camper and hooking it to the utilities. He needed physical labor.

Feeling her anger slowly subside, Ginny saw Michael and Brett leaning against the barn and watching Robert put the finishing touches on the outhouse.

"Hey guys, can you help me?" she asked.

"Sure, Aunt Ginny, what do you need?" Brett asked.

"Come with me." Ginny took them inside to the attic.

Choosing another long portable table, she said, "Take this to the dining room table. Set it up, clean it good and place it opposite the other portable table. It'll make an I shape."

"Okay," they said.

Ginny left the attic and found Leah in the kitchen.

"We may have three more coming," Ginny told her. "Mark invited Ceely's brother and his family to come."

"Thanks for the heads up," Leah replied quietly. "I'll adjust the amount of food on the menus."

"How is the food situation?" Ginny asked. Leah's reaction to more people coming sounded stressed. It mirrored her own concerns.

"Okay for now," Leah answered. "I'll be glad when the summer garden begins to bear. I saw you have a pressure canner in the attic. Do you know how to use it?"

"I do," Ginny said. "I'll teach you. There should be a hot water bath canner up there as well. We can use that for jelly, pickles, and tomatoes."

Mark and Ceely came in the back door.

"What's with the table?" Ceely asked, watching the boys struggle to get the table down the stairs and into the dining room.

"I had Michael and Brett bring another table from the attic," Ginny said. "It will make eating a little more comfortable. Oh, I forgot." Ginny called out to the boys, "Hey guys, could you bring down about four more of the folding chairs from up there too? Thanks."

Looking at Mark, Ginny said, "Tonight will bring our total to twenty-two. I think we're at our limit, Mark. I don't see how we can feed any more people. The kitchen is barely big enough to cook what we need now. Plus, I can see Leah starting to stress over stretching our food resources."

Ginny's phone rang, interrupting the conversation. She apologized, looked at the screen and answered it.

"Hey Tom." Ginny said then paused to listen. She exclaimed, "What! That's terrible." She paused. "Let me talk with Brad and make some arrangements. I'll call you back. We'll try to take care of that today."

"What happened?" Mark asked.

"Someone butchered one of Tom Sutton's steers in the pasture last night," Ginny told them. "It's day four and people are already resorting to theft to eat. He wants to put his cows in one of our pastures for a while in case the thieves come back. I need to go talk to Brad." Ginny left the house, got on the four-wheeler and rode out to the field where Brad was planting corn.

Ceely stood at the door and watched Ginny ride away. She turned and saw her husband staring at the floor.

"What are you thinking, Mark?" Ceely asked.

"I'm thinking it had to have been someone local who knew what Tom had and where they were pastured," Mark replied. "I'm glad those game cameras are going up today. It could be our small herd next."

When Alex and Pete came into the house for lunch, the others were already at the table eating. Pete looked around.

"Where are Ginny and Brad?" he asked.

"Moving cows," Mark said. "Someone butchered one of Tom Sutton's steers right in the pasture last night. They're helping him move his herd onto our pasture for a while. Tom is going to set up game cameras to see if anyone comes back."

"Must have been a local," Pete said. He sat at his usual place at the dining table with a bowl of soup and a sandwich. "It's too soon for wandering refugees to get this far out into the country."

"That's what I thought," Mark replied. "Maybe those cameras will give us a clue."

Not long after lunch, Ceely's brother, Mike, and his wife, Heather, drove up. Their pickup was full, and they were pulling an enclosed trailer behind them. Michael Young climbed out of the truck. A self-employed contractor, he had dark hair and dark, almond shaped eyes.

Heather, Mike's petite wife with blonde hair and blue eyes, was an elementary school teacher. She opened the back seat door and got their two-year-old son, Jackson, from his car seat. Mark was surprised when he saw another truck follow Mike up the drive and stop. A tall man with light brown hair got out and looked around.

Ceely gave her brother and sister-in-law a big hug.

"I'm so glad you're here," she said.

Mike shook Mark's hand and said, "I appreciate this, Mark. We were fine where we were, but we knew it could only be temporary."

The man who got out of the second truck walked up to the group.

Mark," Mike said, "this is Heather's brother, Bennett Grimes. He went with us to Stone Mountain."

"Nice to meet you, Bennett," Mark said as he shook Bennett's hand. "Welcome."

"Thanks. It's nice to meet you, too," Bennett replied. "I appreciate your letting me tag along with your family."

"Now that you're here, you're family, too, Bennett," Mark said. "There are now twenty-three of us staying here. You'll meet everyone at dinner. No matter what, we all eat breakfast and dinner together. Lunch is always at noon, but sometimes people eat at odd times because of what they're doing."

"Do you own this farm, Mark?" Bennett asked. "It's a beautiful place."

"No. My brothers, Garrett and Brad, and I sold our shares of the farm to our sister, Ginny. She and Brad are out helping a neighbor move some cows. Ginny is a veterinarian and farmer. Brad is a chemist and farmer."

"Mom and Dad had friends who lived in the city and liked to come out every summer with their kids," Mark said. "They brought their campers, had bonfires, fished in the pond, played in the creek. It was great for the kids. We loved it too, and we're all still friends. But that's why the RV sites are here with full hookups."

Later that afternoon, Ginny and Brad returned from helping Tom move his cows into their pasture. Dusty and dirty, they had just enough time to shower and put on clean clothes before everyone gathered for the evening meal.

At dinner, everyone was introduced to Mike, Heather, Jackson, and Bennett. The young girls immediately took Jackson outside to play after they ate.

After dinner, Brad built a fire in the fire pit, and everyone sat around it to enjoy a quiet evening. Some people sat together having quiet conversations. Others sat, watching the fire, and listening to the sounds of the farm getting ready for the night. The cows were lowing in the pasture, birds were chirping as they roosted in the trees, and the chickens were moving into the coop's enclosure for the night.

Pete, Mark, and Alex sat with Ginny by the fire and asked, "Were you able to tell anything from the steer carcass?"

"Yes," she said. "It was stabbed in the heart. Died immediately, thank goodness. They took the rumps, the shoulders, and a hunk of rib meat. For someone stealing meat, they left a lot behind, but they knew what they were doing. I imagine it took them only about fifteen minutes to complete the job."

"I think it was someone local," Mark said.

"Is there anyone nearby who works at a butcher shop, restaurant, or grocery store meat department?" Pete asked.

"Not that I know of, but someone nearby could have a friend who does," Ginny answered.

"True," Mark agreed. "We'll just have to wait and see if Tom's game cameras show anything."

The four continued to talk quietly while they watched the children roast marshmallows. Eventually, Mark reminded his daughter to get the other girls and put the chickens up then go get ready for bed. The girls did as they were told and squealed goodnight to Jackson as they ran into the house.

"I think they run everywhere and shout every word," Ginny said, laughing. Ceely, Barbara, and Leah agreed as they got up to make sure their children settled down for the night.

Ginny gave a small sigh of contentment as she watched the flames in the fire pit and scratched Barf behind the ears. She gave a prayer of thanks for this peaceful moment and hoped there would be more peace than anxiety in the coming days.

CHAPTER 21

APRIL 14

In the dim light of predawn, Ginny tiptoed down the stairs. She picked up a cup and poured steaming coffee into it then went into the den where Pete was monitoring the pictures from the game cameras.

"Thanks for making the coffee," she said as she sat in the folding chair beside him. "Is all quiet on the eastern front?"

"Yes, for which I'm grateful," Pete said, smiling. The two sat in companionable silence.

"Did you get to meet Ceely's family?" he asked her.

"Yes," she said, "but I didn't talk with them much. It was a busy afternoon."

"What did you think of Bennett?" Pete asked.

"He seemed fine. Why? Is there a problem?" Ginny asked.

"No. Not at all," Pete replied reassuringly. "I just wonder what his story is. He's quiet, keeps to himself, watches everything and everybody. If I had to guess, I'd say he's been in the military and had some type of extra training, like a Raider or Seal. My assumption is that he's quietly dangerous, and I would not want to be on the wrong side of him. He's offered to take a night shift watching the cameras. Mark is going to put him on the schedule."

"Speaking of that," Ginny said, "Mark has refused to put me on the schedule. He says I'm unpredictable since people call me at all hours to take care of animal emergencies. I think those calls will dwindle as things worsen. Have you seen any news this morning?"

"No," Pete said. "I haven't had the television on. I didn't want to be distracted. Turn it on if you want."

Ginny turned on the television and flipped through the stations until she found the national news.

"Oh, no," Ginny said.

"What?" Pete asked.

"The terrorists struck again," Ginny said as she looked at her phone. There had been no emergency alerts. She looked back at the television. "Bombs were detonated in Wichita, St. Louis, Dallas, New Orleans, Pittsburgh, and Chicago, again. Also, they hit two large power plants in the northeast, but not nuclear plants. The pictures are awful." She turned to Pete who was still watching the computer. "Were you able to find out if your condo was damaged?"

"I was finally able to contact a neighbor," he answered. "My condo didn't take a direct hit, but a dirty bomb was detonated about five miles away."

"I'm sorry, Pete," Ginny said. "I know you think about those people and your home. It must be awful to be so displaced."

"It would be awful if I were trying to survive alone in a strange town. I am quite blessed to have connected with Alex and Mark and met you," Pete said with a smile.

"I'm glad you're here, too," she said smiling. The two simultaneously held up their fists. The fist bump was quickly becoming a tradition when they agreed. Ginny heard a knock at the back door. Bennett stood waiting to be admitted into the house.

"Come in, Bennett," Ginny said as she opened the back door. "Please don't feel like you need permission to come into the house.

The back door will stay unlocked for any of you who need to get in."

"Thank you," Bennett said. "I'll remember that. Any coffee ready?"

"Sure. I'll show you." Ginny showed Bennett where the cups and the coffee pot were along with the cream and sugar.

"Thanks," he said. "I drink it black."

Ginny looked at him, smiled, and said, "Why does that not surprise me?"

Bennett smiled back, "I guess I look like a black coffee kind of guy." He looked across the kitchen and into the den to the computer where Pete was sitting.

"Good morning," he said as he walked over to look at the monitor. "Would you explain what you have here?"

Pete picked up an aerial map of the farm and showed Bennett where the game cameras were, why they were up, about the Sutton's steer, and about the Johnsons being so close to the road.

"That's not good." Everyone turned to see Mark standing in the den, watching the television. "Terrorists have hit us again. They've ruined cities and killed people, but all we have done is a drone attack that only hit military missile sites."

"I have a friend who knows the right people," Bennett said. "He told me the CIA has traced most of the bomb residue to China, Iran, and Russia. If it were me, I'd get our people out of those places, and lull those governments into a false sense of security. Then, as soon as I had everyone out and everything in place, they wouldn't know what hit them. But that's me. I'm not a diplomat." Bennett paused then said, "What's not common information it that some of the residue can be linked to Brazil and South Africa."

"BRICS nations," Pete said quietly. He looked at Bennett who nodded. Pete's respect for Bennett's training, connections, and discretion increased. Bennett probably had that information for several days.

"Looks like the President is going to speak," Garrett said, looking at his phone as he joined the group.

The adults, all dressed for another day of work, stood around the television watching the news report. Adam and Barbara were in the kitchen mixing batter and cooking panakes. Pete listened while he kept his eyes on the security cameras' live feed.

Pete stiffened as he saw a black pickup truck pass under one of the cameras on the paved road. It drove south but didn't stop anywhere within the range of the cameras. Pete froze a frame with the truck on it. He looked around and caught Ginny's eye and motioned her over to the computer. He showed her the picture.

"Do you know anyone with a pickup like that?" he asked. "Is that truck where it's supposed to be or is it someone from outside the community."

"I don't recognize it," Ginny said, "but then I don't know everyone who lives in this area. Plus, it could be someone from somewhere else coming to stay with family. It's hard to say."

"Will you call Aaron Johnson and see if he saw it?" Pete asked. "It was headed in their direction."

"Sure." Ginny took her cell phone to the front porch to call her neighbor.

A few minutes later, Ginny came back into the room and sat beside Pete.

"Aaron said Carson saw it," Ginny told him. "They put game cameras up, too. The truck slowed down in front of their house, but it kept going. Carson saw it again on the feed from the cameras they put at the Smith farm. They rent that land and wanted to keep an eye on the house. The truck pulled into the drive. A man got out and went into the house. Aaron thinks it's one of the Smith children, because he had a key. He didn't break in.

"Anyway, he said the man stayed only about ten minutes then left. Aaron said the man was empty handed when he left, so he wonders if the family is going to try to come here. He thinks they're in the

Winston Salem area, because that's where he sends his rent checks. Aaron has a key to the house that the Smith's gave him so he could watch over the place. He's going to go over there later this morning and see if he can determine what that man did inside."

"Okay," Pete said, "that makes sense and eases my mind a bit. There's almost no traffic on the road and any vehicle at all stands out. It should be easy to spot trouble."

Mark, Alex, and Bennett noticed Ginny and Pete pointing to the screen. They gathered around the two to look at the computer screen.

"Everything peaceful?" Mark asked.

"This guy slowed down at the Johnsons," Pete said, pointing to the pickup, "but he moved on and pulled into the Smith farm. He went into the house, but he didn't break in. Evidently, he had a key. Aaron is going to check the house out this morning to see if he can tell what's going on there."

"The Smith kids must be Garrett's age or older," Ginny said. "I barely remember them. I'll have Aaron see if Carson can freeze a picture of the guy and text it to me. We can show it to Garrett."

Ginny took her cell phone back to the porch. When she came back in, she had a picture of the man who had been in the house. The image was clear but distant. Mark had Garrett look at the picture.

"I only remember them as kids and teens," Garrett said, "but that guy looks just like Mr. Smith. I would say it's his son."

"Thanks," Ginny said. "I'll let Aaron know." Ginny went back to the front porch to make her call.

At eight the group gathered for breakfast, and Brett relieved Pete at the computer. When everyone had finished eating, Ginny demonstrated the use of the solar showers and said the outdoor shower would be finished by the end of the day. Anyone who used it was required to refill the containers with water and hang them on the outside of the shower to warm in the sun.

At lunch Brad reported that he had gotten some information from a friend. The grocery stores in Elkin were closed. The mayor and chief of police had decided that all the food left at the stores in town would be gathered in City Hall and guarded by the police to prevent looting. They're saying that they're protecting the citizens' welfare by taking all the food to one place like that. The mayor says he has coordinated with the businesses so that they can be paid appropriately. People needing groceries were to call the city office for an appointment to shop. All grocery trucks would take their loads to that location. Also, the Governor signed an executive order declaring a state of emergency and that everyone should shelter in place.

"That won't be easy to enforce," Robert said. "Plus, I wouldn't want to be working at the City Hall today. Can you imagine calling to shop for groceries and being told your first appointment was in three days or more?"

"Yeah," Brad agreed. "Plus, my friend said that the people in Elkin are not happy about this. The owners and managers of the stores tried to refuse, but the police took the food anyway. Also, if the stores receive shipments instead of directing them to City Hall, the managers will be arrested for hoarding food and supplies."

"That's awful!" exclaimed Ginny. "It's more than awful, it's corrupt."

"They're excusing their actions by saying they don't have enough police to guard every store," Brad said, "and some looting did occur before they started this."

"I'm so glad we aren't in Greensboro," Erica said. "If this is going on there, we would starve to death in our apartment." She looked at Ginny, "Thank you for letting us stay here." Everyone else chimed in with their own thanks.

"You're all welcome here," Ginny said with a smile. She felt her anxiety lessen. No matter how hard it might get, she was glad she had not turned anyone away.

CHAPTER 22
APRIL 15

Ginny quietly went downstairs, looking forward to her morning coffee. Walking through the den to the kitchen, she glanced over to see Bennett at the computers, an empty coffee cup on the desk.

"Need a refill?" she asked as she walked toward him.

"Sure." Bennett held his coffee cup out for her to fill. "Thanks."

Ginny smiled and took his cup. She refilled it and poured herself a cup of coffee. After taking a careful sip of her own hot liquid, she took Bennett's cup to the desk and set it down beside him.

"All quiet?" she asked.

"Yes," he said, "and that's a good thing."

"Agreed," Ginny said as she sat in the folding chair beside his. "Mark said you taught classes at an outdoor store. What did you teach?"

"Some bow and arrow shooting, firearms classes, and the occasional tent camping demonstrations," Bennett replied. "I mostly stocked shelves or ran the cash register. It was only part time. I have a very small retirement benefit from the military. I was in the Marines. But mostly Heather and I have trust funds we inherited when our parents died. She likes teaching so she still does that. You should have her hold classes for the kids. It's only been a few days, but we don't know how long this will last, and they should keep learning."

"You're exactly right," Ginny replied. "I'll suggest that to Mark. If you haven't noticed, he's the unofficial head of this place. I may own it, but he's coordinating our response to this emergency. He was an officer in the army, and I think he's organizing things like he ran his platoon. Regardless, it's working so far. I couldn't do what he does. Mark, Pete, and Alex all served together. They're pretty tight friends, but not exclusive."

Bennett started to reply but stopped, stiffened and concentrated on the monitor. The black pickup was back and going in the same direction.

"I'll call Aaron," Ginny said and took her phone to the front porch.

A few minutes later, Ginny came back into the den. Mark, Garrett, Pete and Alex were standing at the computer talking with Bennett.

"Carson said it pulled back into the Smith's driveway again," Ginny told Bennett, "but this time the bed of the truck was piled high with bins and suitcases. The man, a woman, and two kids unloaded the truck and went inside. Aaron is getting ready to go over there."

"One of us needs to go with him," Bennett said.

"I'll go," Garrett said. "We may know each other. He'll probably know Aaron, but two friendly faces may make him feel better."

Ginny called and suggested the plan to Aaron.

She turned to Garrett and said, "Aaron will pick you up in fifteen minutes."

Adam came to the computer to relieve Bennett.

"We need to follow them," Bennett said to Mark. "We don't have to be seen, but we need to make sure those people are reasonable and won't shoot first. We can take my truck." Mark agreed.

A few minutes later, Garrett climbed into Aaron's pickup. As soon as they were out of the drive, Bennett and Mark followed at a distance.

They parked on the side of the road where they could watch the Smith house but couldn't be seen by anyone at the house.

Bennett and Mark watched as the man came out and shook hands with Aaron and Garrett. They talked for a while, then Aaron and Garrett got back into Aaron's truck. Bennett did a U-turn and drove back to the house.

Aaron dropped Garrett off at the farm and drove back to his own house. Garrett told the group that it was Rob Smith, a member of the family who owned the farm and that he was glad to know who was living nearby.

A few minutes later Ginny got a text. She laughed and went to show Mark and Bennett the image that had caught them spying on Aaron and Garrett. Garrett looked at the picture then at Mark and Bennett; he thanked them for being there.

After supper, couples and family groups gathered around the fire pit. Everyone was tired. Even the teenagers sat quietly with their families. Ginny was staring into the fire.

"You look pensive," Pete said, placing an outdoor chair beside hers and sitting down. "Anything wrong?"

"I don't know," she answered. "I have a bad feeling in my gut that something's about to happen. I don't know if it's here or across the Pacific, but I just have a feeling."

"I learned in the army to listen to that feeling," Pete said nodding. "It's like a second sense. You should learn to trust it, especially after all that's been happening. All we can do is wait and see what develops. I have the watch from twelve to four at the computer. If it's going to be here, that's usually the time of night criminals like to work. I'll keep my eyes open. If I see anything, I will text you. Does that help?"

Ginny smiled. "Yes. Thank you."

CHAPTER 23

APRIL 16

Ginny woke up to complete darkness. She looked at the clock on her bedside table; it was three in the morning. She couldn't sleep, and she didn't want to wake Holly who was still sleeping on the other side of the king sized bed. Knowing Pete would be sitting at the computer, Ginny quietly got dressed and went downstairs to see what was happening.

"Anything going on?" she asked and sat down beside him.

"Nope," he said, "just a few deer, one raccoon, and what I think was a skunk."

Ginny giggled. "That's tame for a night in the country. What is that?" Ginny asked, pointing to the monitor that showed a figure walking on the road.

Pete calmly zoomed in on the figure and said, "That is a person. We have our first real alert." Pete zoomed out to watch. "He's walking north. He passed the Johnson's and is now in front of our drive." Pete froze a frame and sent a copy of the person to his phone.

"Look at this," Pete said, pointing to the picture. "He's wearing a backpack. This is a person on the move and probably only walks at night. I don't think he's anyone we need to worry about. He isn't looking around or slowing down. This guy has a plan and is moving on."

"Should I call Tom?" Ginny asked. "His farm is the next place on the road going north."

"I hate to wake him, but it wouldn't hurt," Pete said.

Ginny pulled Tom from her contacts and pushed the call button.

"Hello?" Tom answered sleepily.

"Tom, this is Ginny Reed. I'm sorry to wake you up in the middle of the night, but we spotted someone walking on the road. He passed us and should be passing your place about now. We wanted you to know."

Tom was instantly alert. "I'll watch the road. Thanks for calling." Ginny was about to hang up when she heard a door slam, and Tom suddenly started laughing. "Ginny that was my boy. He made it home from Charlotte."

"Oh, Tom, I'm so glad. I'll let you go. Happy reunion." Ginny ended the call and with tears in her eyes, she looked at Pete, "That was Tom's son who has been trying to get home from Charlotte. Tom is so happy."

"I'm glad," Pete said. "That was a good alert. I hope that's all we have. Do you think that was what you were feeling?"

Ginny sobered. "No. That would have been anticipation of something. This is dread." A news alert sounded on Ginny's phone.

"I guess this is what I was feeling," she said and starting reading the news release. "North Korea started bombing Seoul. The number of conventional missiles hitting the city per minute was horrible. The city is almost demolished. Then they invaded. South Korea responded by bombing Pyongyang. North Korea bombed Camp Humphreys. Then South Korea bombed a military airfield in North Korea." Ginny opened another news site on her phone.

"It gets worse," she said. "The terrorists struck again. This time they used tactical weapons. They hit NORAD and nuclear missile silos in Montana, North Dakota, and Nebraska. They also struck a military communications station in Maine. I can't imagine they did any damage to NORAD, but they hit and disabled some of our nuclear weapons, and we have no idea who did it. A total of fifteen terrorist groups are taking credit. And still we do nothing," she added sarcastically.

Pete reached over and rubbed Ginny's neck and shoulders. He had noticed that was where she tensed and felt stress. Ginny relaxed and let Pete's fingers smooth the knots in her neck.

"You do that so well," she said. "Where did you learn that helpful skill?"

"Practice," he said. "I used to do it for my mom. She was a single parent and had a lot of stress. Then I helped some of the guys work out sore muscles in the army."

Ginny grinned, "Well, if you ever need your hoofs trimmed or a rabies shot, I'll return the favor."

The back door opened and Bennett came into the house to relieve Pete. He went straight to the coffee pot and poured himself a cup of coffee from the carafe sitting on a hot plate. He took a sip as he walked over to the computer.

Pete got up and let Bennett have his seat. After taking a few steps, he stretched his muscles, rubbing his lower back.

"Good night, Pete," Ginny said. "Have a good sleep and thank you for the neck rub."

"My pleasure, Ginny," Pete said with a smile. "You need to go back to bed, yourself. You work too hard to be sleep deprived."

"I know," Ginny said with a yawn. "Now that I know why I woke up, maybe I can get back to sleep. But I think I will just curl up on the couch so I don't wake Holly up."

"I saw the news on my phone," Bennett said, settling into the desk chair. "Is that what you're talking about?"

"Probably," Ginny said. "I woke up about three with a feeling of dread that something was about to happen, and then we got those notifications. I hope there's nothing else."

"That's interesting," Bennett said. "If you ever wake up with winning lottery numbers, let me know."

Ginny giggled. "Oh, hush, you. I wish that would happen." Ginny walked to the couch, laid down and covered herself with a soft blanket in hues of sage green. "Good night, Pete. Good night, Bennett."

"Good night, Ginny," the two men said. Pete went to his room and Bennett turned back to the monitors.

Just before she fell asleep, Ginny said loud enough for Bennett to hear, "Pete and I saw a man walking down the road earlier. He was the son of a neighbor who had been trying to home from Charlotte. We forgot to tell you."

"Thanks." Bennett answered.

Bennett turned and saw that Ginny was asleep then turned back to the monitor. He was glad she was resting. Bennett admitted that he found her intriguing. She had to be one of the smartest and nicest people he'd ever met. He also saw that there was something between her and Pete. *Good for them.*

Ginny's internal clock woke her at dawn. She looked at her phone, which was lying on the floor beside her. It was six o'clock, and there were no notifications to give her more bad news. Bennett was sitting at the monitors, quiet but alert.

"Good morning, Bennett," she said sleepily.

"Morning, Ginny," he replied. "I heard you wake up but decided I'd better keep my eye on the camera feed. Things can pass by in a hurry."

"How many deer did you see?" she asked.

Bennett smiled, "Six since the sky started to lighten."

Pete came into the den.

"Good morning. Everything quiet, Bennett?" he asked.

"Yes," Bennett answered. "Quiet and boring. Just the way I like it."

Pete sat in the chair beside Bennett. While they talked, Ginny slipped upstairs to change clothes. When she came back down, Erica was fixing breakfast and Michael had relieved Bennett at the computer. Garrett and Mark were standing outside the office talking with Brad. She walked over to join them.

"Is this an exclusive conversation or can the other Reed sibling join?" she asked.

Garrett put his arm around Ginny and pulled her into the group.

"We were just talking about church," he said. "It's Sunday. We need to take the time to be grateful and to pray the farm."

"You're right," Ginny agreed. "I take it you've thought this through. How do you want to do it?"

"After breakfast. Near the fire pit," Garrett said. "We can arrange the chairs on one side of it, and I'll stand on the other. It will be short, but I think it will be on point for what we're dealing with. Then I want all of us to join hands to pray the farm."

"I like it," Ginny said. "I hope you've made yourself our unofficial pastor, shepherd, and counselor. You're good at that."

"I didn't know you thought that," Garrett said, his eyebrows raised with surprise.

"Of course, Garrett," Ginny said. "I notice things. Even though you are several years older than I am, I noticed your character. Mark, Brad, and I all noticed. You were as much a role model to us as Mom and Dad were."

"I had no idea," Garrett said, tears filling his eyes. Blinking hard, Garrett pulled his brothers and sister in for a group hug. "I love you all and appreciate every strength and talent you bring to this moment. Ginny, I appreciate you and Brad keeping this farm a haven for us all. Now, let's eat breakfast."

When everyone had eaten, Garrett announced that anyone who wanted to participate could come to the backyard for a short, informal worship service. He also told them that they would take the rest of the day off.

While the kitchen was being cleaned, people changed out of their work clothes. Parents gathered their children and went outside. Bennett went to relieve Michael at the computer.

"Don't you want to go to church?" Michael asked.

"Michael," Bennett said, "God and I have been on good terms for longer than you've been alive. You need to go be with your family. When it's over, come back and take your place."

"Yes, Sir," Michael said and went to find his family. Bennett watched the young man walk outside and thought how impressive all three of those boys were.

Garrett gave a short talk on their current situation and how easy it is to live in fear. Then he gave them scripture references on how to lean on God and give up that fear. When he was finished, everyone held hands while he thanked God for their blessings and asked for their continued safety.

When the short service was over, everyone put their fold-up chairs in the equipment shed. Just as soon as they had gotten back into the house, rain started pounding on the metal roof of the house. The rain lasted off and on all day, forcing them inside to read, rest, watch movies, and take their Sunday off.

CHAPTER 24

APRIL 17

Ginny woke before dawn, covered in sweat. That anxious feeling of dread was back. She wasn't surprised. The circumstances were enough to give the most confident of people anxiety. She dressed and went downstairs where she found Bennett watching the computer.

"Good morning," Ginny said as she walked to the kitchen. "You seem to be permanently attached to this shift."

"I'm an early riser," Bennett replied. "This is just a usual morning for me. You seem to get up before everyone, too. Is that normal for you?"

"I suppose," she answered while pouring herself a cup of coffee. "Sometimes I think my whole circadian rhythm is off balance. My job has me out at crazy hours sometimes."

"But you love it," Bennett observed.

"That is correct," Ginny said smiling. "I wouldn't do anything else."

"Good morning," Pete said as he walked into the den from his room. "Is everything quiet?"

"It was," Bennett answered and pointed to the monitor. "Look at this."

Pete looked over Bennett's shoulder. An old red pickup truck was moving slowly down the road. It stopped at Ginny's driveway then moved on, slowly going to the Johnson's and turning into their drive.

"Ginny," Bennett said, already getting out of the chair, "watch the monitors and call the Johnson's. Pete, come with me. We'll take my truck. I have a very bad feeling about this."

Bennett and Pete ran out of the house to Bennett's truck. He started the engine and raced out of the drive before Ginny finished dialing Aaron's number.

"Hello," answered a sleepy voice.

"Aaron, this is Ginny. There's a truck in your drive. Do you recognize it?"

Aaron was immediately alert, and Ginny heard the sound of blinds being pulled up at the window.

"We don't recognize it. Do you know who it is?" Aaron asked.

"No, but Pete and Bennett are on the way," Ginny told him. "They're in Bennett's truck, which is dark gray, and they're pulling into your driveway now."

Bennett stopped at the end of the Johnson's drive and watched the red truck.

"Pete," he said, "behind the seat, hand me the rifle. You take the shotgun. No offense, but I know my rifle."

"None taken," Pete replied as he handed Bennett his rifle.

"Open your door and stay behind it," Bennett instructed with an air of confident authority. "If you need to shoot, do it in the gap between the door and cab, but stay behind the door. It's bulletproofed." The two men eased their doors open.

Aaron came out on the front porch. The sun was just starting to come up, but he was able to see Pete and Bennett's gun barrels.

"Can I help you?" Aaron called to the red pickup, which was sitting quietly in the driveway.

A young man who looked to be in his upper teens got out.

"I came to see Bonnie," he said loudly. "We're friends."

"No one comes calling at six in the morning," Aaron replied, his voice loud and echoing through the yard. "Get back in your truck. Leave and don't come back."

"You really ought to let me see Bonnie, old man," the younger man called out, taking a couple steps toward the porch. "I won't give up."

The driver of the red truck watched the front door open slightly and heard, "Dad, Bonnie doesn't know them or have any idea how they might know her."

"My daughter doesn't know you," Aaron called out. He pulled his pistol from behind his back and pointed it at the man standing by the truck. "I said to leave. You can pull through the yard back to the road."

A second man, about the same age as the driver, got out of the passenger's side. Pete could see that he had a gun in his hand.

"Pistol in the passenger's hand," Pete whispered to Bennett.

"Driver has one in his waistband in back," Bennett answered.

"Come on, now," the first teen said. "I'm Kyle and this is Zach. Bonnie does know me. She's lying if she says she doesn't. Ask her. She'll want to come with me."

Aaron didn't answer. He continued to hold his pistol steady as he stared at the young man.

The tone of Kyle's voice changed to a threatening tone, "This is your last warning. Send the girl out, or you die, and I get Bonnie anyway." Kyle took another step forward, and Zach shifted his position to face Bennett's truck.

"Or you die trying," Aaron answered firmly.

Zach pulled up his gun and fired at Pete while Kyle fired at Aaron. Kyle's bullet missed, but before Kyle could fire a seond shot, Aaron fired his pistol and hit the Kyle in the chest, center mass. At the same time, Bennett shot Kyle in the head. As soon as Zach's bullet bounced off Bennett's truck, Pete moved from behind the truck's door, fired, and filled Zach's head with buckshot. Then it was quiet.

Bennett and Pete approached the rear of the truck from either side. Pete kicked the gun away from the passenger's hand. Bennett did the same for the driver of the truck. Both teens were dead.

"Did you know them?" Pete asked Aaron.

"No," Aaron answered. "Carson said Bonnie doesn't know them either. I didn't think she did, but I'd sure like to know how they knew her and where she lived. I think we all know why they wanted a teenage girl, but I don't want to think about Bonnie being taken by them."

Bonnie started to come out on the porch.

"Stay inside, Bonnie," Aaron said loudly. When Bonnie opened the door again, Aaron said, "Listen to me, Bonnie. Stay inside."

"Daddy, I don't know them. Do you believe me?" Bonnie asked in a pleading tone.

"Yes, Bonnie. I believe you," Aaron said reassuringly. "Could one of them have been connected to your school?"

Carson came out onto the porch then walked to the red truck.

"I knew them," he said quietly so Bonnie couldn't hear him. "Their last name is Howell. Kyle graduated from my school last year. Zach was a year ahead of me but just stopped showing up for classes a few months ago. I never liked them. They always tried to be tough guys, bullies. They and their little group paid no attention to me, so I don't know how they knew I had a sister."

Pete heard a four-wheeler coming through the trees. Mark came around the barn and into the driveway.

"Everything all right?" Mark asked as he got off the four-wheeler. Walking toward the truck, Mark looked at the bodies and the small holes in the truck from the buckshot.

"It is now," Pete said. He pointed to the teens, "Carson knew them as troublemakers at the high school. They were part of the group in the blue pickup I saw in Elkin a few days ago. I especially remember the younger one yelling from the bed of the truck."

"Carson," Aaron said, turning to his son, "would you go to the kitchen and get the latex gloves we keep for treating horses?"

Carson nodded, but his mother had already brought a box of gloves out to the porch. Carson took them and offered them to the men.

"If you'll put these on, we can load the bodies on the back of their truck," Aaron said. "Get their guns and ammo, and we can search their truck for anything of value. Then I'm going to drive it and park it behind an abandoned house about two miles away. The bank owns the farm, but it hasn't been put up for auction."

The men did as Aaron instructed. As they worked, Carson pulled Pete to the side.

"I didn't want to worry Dad or Bonnie," Carson said, "but I'm pretty sure there is a girl in that family just a year older than Bonnie. She and Bonnie are friends, but not real close like Bonnie is with some other girls. Bonnie doesn't know her friend is related to these guys, and I don't want her to know."

"That would explain how they knew about Bonnie," Pete said. "Thanks for the information." Carson nodded.

Soon, Aaron was ready to drive the truck down the road. He turned to the three men from the Reed farm.

"Thanks for coming," he said. "It would have ended differently if you hadn't been here." Worry was etched in Aaron's features. "When these two don't return, I'm afraid others will come looking for them. They know where we live and that there is a teenage girl here."

"What about moving to the apartment over your barn?" Pete asked. "No one can see it from here."

"It's only got room for two," Aaron said. "We have six people here, now."

Mark took a deep breath and said, "There's an extra RV site at our place. Why don't you move your camper there for your sister-in-law,

Bonnie and her cousin. Carson can bunk with the boys. That would leave just you and Donna to stay in the apartment. I think you're right. I think you'll have more visitors when these two don't return."

Aaron suddenly looked relieved.

"Will that be okay?" he asked. "I'm afraid we won't be as lucky next time if these guys have friends who come looking for them. Plus, my animals are back there, and I can guard them better if I'm closer to them."

"Sure," Mark answered. "Let's plan on that. I'll let Ginny know."

Aaron shook Mark's hand, "Thank you."

"You're welcome," Mark replied. "I'll go on back and tell Ginny."

Mark started the four-wheeler and rode back to the farm. He dreaded the conversation he was about to have with Ginny, but he didn't see any other way to keep the Johnson family safe, especially since they had two teenage girls living there.

After Mark left, the bodies were loaded into the bed of the red truck. Aaron opened the driver's door to get in. He grimaced. The odor of beer and stale food was strong.

"We'll follow you and bring you back," Bennett said. He and Pete got in their truck, and Bennett backed out of the driveway.

Aaron backed the truck out of his driveway and flipped down the visor to block the early morning sun. The whole episode had lasted less than hour, but it seemed longer. He drove about two miles south and turned into an abandoned farm. He parked the truck behind the house then walked back to the road and climbed into the back seat of Bennett's truck.

"Thank you," he said.

"Are you all right?" Pete asked. "It isn't everyday someone tries to kill you, and you have to kill them."

"I am glad about that, but I'll be fine. I threw up the nerves behind the house. Quite unmanly of me," he said grinning.

Pete and Bennett gave him knowing smiles.

"Not at all, Aaron" Pete said. "We would worry if you hadn't."

When they returned to the Johnson farm, Pete asked, "Do you need help moving the girls over?"

"Probably not," Aaron replied. "I'll move the camper now. We can pack everything in Grace's SUV, and I'll drive Bonnie and Hannah over."

"All right. Just give us a call when you're coming. After today we may make our driveway inaccessible," Pete said.

Chapter 25

April 17

Mark returned to Ginny's house and parked the four-wheeler at the equipment shed. When he walked back into the house, he saw that Robert had replaced Ginny at the computer.

Ginny walked over to Mark and quietly asked, "What happened? You look very serious."

Mark took Ginny by the arm and led her toward the back door. He motioned for Alex to follow. In the yard, Mark told Ginny and Alex what had happened.

"Ginny," Mark said, "I'm sorry, but I told Aaron he could park his camper here. There's enough room in it for the girls and Donna's sister. Carson will bunk here with the boys. That leaves Donna and Aaron, who will stay in the apartment over the barn."

"Those guys knew Bonnie lived there," Mark said, looking directly at Ginny. "They're dead, but when they don't return, their friends will come looking for them."

"He's right, Ginny," Alex said. "Holly described that tight-knit group of guys who liked to cause trouble before all this chaos. I imagine they're loving this situation and taking advantage of the state of emergency and the resulting panic. Also, if they're family, then someone is sure to come for revenge."

Ginny looked at Mark, shocked that he hadn't kept his promise to consult her before bringing more people to the farm. She started to get angry but just gave a resigned sigh. He had done the right thing.

"You were right, Mark," she said. "Letting the Johnson's live here is the safest thing right now. Jerks like that will be angry if they think their friends were killed. They could very well retaliate against Aaron's family. When are they moving?"

Mark replied, "Today. I expect Aaron to drive up with his camper at any time.

The three heard tires rolling over gravel and turned around to see Bennett's truck. Bennett parked, and he and Pete got out of the cab.

As they were walking toward the others, Mark asked them, "Is everything taken care of?"

"Yes," Pete said. "Aaron hid the truck behind an old abandoned farmhouse. The whole family is pretty shaken up by this."

He looked at Ginny, "Did Mark tell you they're going to move over here?"

"Yes," Ginny said, nodding. "It's the safest solution. There's no way I want to risk that family getting hurt or killed if those guys have friends who come looking for them."

"Yeah," Pete said. "The Johnson's are nice people."

"When are they coming?" she asked.

"As soon as they can get the camper here and their belongings moved over," Pete answered. "Donna and Aaron are moving to the barn apartment and will take their valuables from the house."

"I'd better go downstairs and make sure there's a clean bunk for Carson and room for his clothes," Ginny said. "Those boys have their stuff scattered all over that room." She turned and walked toward the house.

The men watched her go inside the house. Pete waited for the back door screen to slam shut before turning to Mark.

"What did she say about your asking more people over here?" Pete asked. "She's generous, but she still worries about so many people being here. She feels responsible for everyone."

"She seemed okay with it," Mark replied. "She said she would rather have them here than leave them there and in danger of retaliation from that gang."

"She's a strong woman with a good heart," Alex observed. The other men agreed.

That afternoon, Aaron brought his camper over. Grace, Bonnie and Hannah had already put their belongings in it, but they brought boxes of food and paper products into the house from Grace's SUV. Carson carried his few bags to the room with the other boys in the basement.

When the camper was in place, Aaron said to Mark, "I have enough plywood to board my place up. Carson and I could use some help nailing it up, especially on the first floor. I wouldn't put it past the friends of those guys to shoot my house up just for the sake of revenge."

Mark's brother-in-law, Mike, volunteered to help Aaron and took his trailer with his tools. Robert, Michael, Brett and Adam also went to help.

Ginny made sure Grace and the girls were introduced to everyone. When Heather found out that Grace was a teacher, she pulled Grace to the side and discussed lesson plans for teaching the high schoolers. Ginny was glad Grace had found a niche in the group.

Thinking about Bonnie and Hannah, who were fourteen and feeling out of place, Ginny took them to see Leah. She introduced them and told the girls they would be helping Leah with the cooking and her husband, Robert, with the garden.

Ginny changed the dining arrangements. She put the card table away. The teenagers would eat at a long portable table in the den. The younger children would eat at the breakfast nook. She added three chairs to the adult table, one each for Grace, Donna, and Aaron. Ginny called Aaron to let them know they had a place at the table for all meals now.

That evening Aaron carried a gallon of milk into the kitchen. Donna had a pound of butter in a plastic bowl and a hunk of cheese wrapped in cloth.

"This is wonderful!" exclaimed Leah. "How did you know we were running low on dairy products?"

"I'm glad we could contribute," Donna said. "We have a cow, and we don't drink all the milk every day. That's why I make butter and cheese, but with this many people, it may take all the milk to cook and give the children some to drink."

Mark came into the kitchen from the front porch. He was surprised to see Aaron.

"Hey," he said. "I didn't hear you two drive up."

"We have a golf cart," Aaron said, grinning. "It makes no noise. The apartment over the barn is too far away to walk, especially in bad weather. So, we thought we'd get used to driving it over. Our place looks deserted, and we don't want any noise to change that impression."

"I assume you've been watching your game cameras. Any activity?" Mark asked, his voice rising above the chaos in the kitchen. The kids were running around claiming they were hungry. Adults were coming in from outside and washing up in the mudroom.

"Not yet," Aaron answered, his voice rising to match Mark's. "Not even a drive by. Those two must not have very loyal friends. I would've been tearing up the road by now if my friends hadn't come back."

Donna and Grace stood back, watching everything and wondering if they would adjust to this level of noise at Ginny's house. The Johnson house had been almost silent compared to this.

Finally, the food was ready and Mark quieted the group with his characteristic whistle. Introductions were made, the blessing was said, and everyone had dinner.

Ginny had just finished her meal when her phone rang. Mark was sitting across from her and stopped eating to listen.

"This is Dr. Reed." She listened then asked, "Did they see who it was? Did your cameras show anything?" Ginny paused then said, "Brad checks on them twice a day let me ask."

Ginny looked at Brad, "Are all of the cows still in the pasture?"

"Yes. Full count of both his and ours before supper," Brad informed her.

Ginny returned to her conversation, "Tom, all the cows are safe in the pasture. None are missing. Keep us posted if you learn anything or see anything on your cameras, and we'll let you know if we see anything. Thanks."

Ginny ended the call and saw everyone was looking at her expectantly.

"The Millers across the road from Tom had a steer butchered in their pasture last night," she said as she laid her phone back on the table. "Tom said they called the sheriff, but they haven't heard from him or any deputies. Tom also said he hasn't seen anybody on his game cameras. The common factor for both farms is that the cows were in a pasture near the road. The Millers have moved theirs to another pasture farther back and placed game cameras along the road, too."

"The sheriff's department may be stretched thin," Donna said.

"Or they know who it is, and they're protecting them," Alex said.

"We saw that happen a lot when we were deployed," Pete added. "The local law enforcement became feudal lords in some cases."

"That's all we need," Garrett said with a groan. "That's like the fox guarding the hen house."

"Well, we don't know for sure, so there's no need to borrow trouble," Ginny said. "I know the sheriff and most of the deputies. I've taken care of their animals. I can't imagine they would stoop this low."

"But these aren't normal times, Ginny," Mark said. "We hope that they're above theft, especially one as brutal as this, but men desperate to feed their families won't think a thing about stealing food."

Robert sat in front of the computer trying to eat spaghetti neatly while keeping his eyes on the computer. He stopped eating, stiffened and froze a picture.

"Mark," he called.

Mark got up and sat in the extra chair beside Robert. Robert clicked the mouse and brought up the picture of a blue pickup truck.

"This truck just drove past us going toward Aaron's place," he said.

Mark looked back at Aaron, who was looking at his cell phone. Aaron got up and joined them in front of the computer.

"They slowed down in front of the house, but they kept going," Aaron said as he watched the pictures on his phone from all the cameras he had placed around his house and the Smith house. "They must have turned around because they came back," he said, "and they're driving very slowly past the house. You should see them soon."

"Yeah. Got 'em," Robert said. "Looks like they're picking up speed and moving on. They didn't hesitate at our driveway."

Mark looked at Aaron, "Looks like we got you and your family moved out of your house just in time. Your place looks deserted. Hopefully those guys will never know what happened to their friends."

After a slight pause, Mark said, "Tomorrow the mailbox comes out and our driveway made impassable. We can use the gate at the clinic if we need to leave. This mess could last a long time, and we don't know what kind of trouble could come our way. Aaron, we need to do the same to your drive and front yard. Any ideas?"

Mike had joined the group. "I have a few pieces of rebar in the trailer and a tool that will cut them. We can make a sharp point on one end then bury them at an angle to blow any tires coming up the drive. Once the grass grows up, you won't be able to see the spikes. But I don't think I have enough to go across a whole yard. We could do the same with treated lumber, though. It won't last as long, but it would give protection for a while."

"Thank you, Mike. We'll do that in the morning," Mark said.

"I have some two by fours," Aaron said. "A few of those across the yard with twenty penny nails sticking up through them won't be pretty but will stop a truck. I can anchor them to the ground with barbed wire and stakes. Let the grass grow, and they'll be hidden."

"Sounds like a plan," Mark said. "We'll start right after breakfast."

That evening, Ginny and Brad were in the office talking quietly when Garrett and Mark joined them.

"What's going on?" asked Mark.

"You know I bought the Thompson farm," Brad said. "Ginny has two game cameras left in the basement. After what happened today, I want to put them around that place, too. Ginny said I could use them. My house isn't as close to the road as Aaron's but it's still visible. Maybe Aaron has enough twenty penny nails that we could protect that drive and yard the same way."

"We'll put all the cameras we have left along that road and your driveway," Mark said. "We'll help you secure the house."

"Ginny," Brad said, "Will you and Holly go over there and take out whatever towels, dishes, and supplies they may have left behind that we could use here?"

"Of course, Brad," Ginny said. "We'll put everything in the basement and label it with your name so they go back when you move in."

Brad gave a sigh of relief. "Thanks."

Chapter 26
April 20

Pete watched the clock. He knew Ginny would be coming down at some point. She usually woke up around 5:30. Then, as if on cue, he heard footsteps tiptoeing lightly down the stairs. He turned around to make sure it was her then turned back to the monitor when he saw her trim body and that her hair was down instead of up in a ponytail. He groaned inwardly. She was wearing those leggings and the long t-shirt that she had been wearing at the airport. She had no idea how good she looked. He wanted to hold her and kiss her, but he knew that would never work. Their situation was unstable, and they were stuck together for the foreseeable future. The last thing he needed to do was make things awkward between them. So, he would settle for coffee and conversation.

Ginny kept track of the computer rotations, and when Pete had the early morning shift, she would rise early and sit with him for a while. She enjoyed their conversations and felt safe with him. If she were honest with herself, she would admit to wondering what it would be like to kiss Peter Flinn, but she didn't want to let her thoughts drift in that direction. So, she settled for coffee and conversation.

"How is everything?" she asked as she passed the computer and walked into the kitchen.

"Quiet," Pete answered. "Did you sleep well?"

"Yes," she said, pouring her daily cup of coffee. "Let me check the news." Ginny turned the television on with the sound low and watched for a few minutes.

Sitting in the empty chair beside Pete, she said, "North and South Korea are still fighting. At least it's with conventional weapons. We've been fortunate to have a few days with no new surprises. I hope that trend continues."

"Me, too." Pete put his arm on the back of her chair and absently ran his fingers through the long strands of her hair that reached below her shoulders. "What's on your agenda for today? You haven't had a vet call in over twenty-four hours. Is that usual?"

"It can be," she answered. "If the clinic was open, I would be busy. But emergency calls usually occur in clusters for some reason. What are you doing today?"

"Alex and I are going to put in fresh backup batteries in the game cameras and make sure they're still secure. We had a lot of wind with the storm last night. We'll put up the last cameras at Brad's place, too, then make sure they're included in the live feed."

Pete continued to watch the monitors. His fingers were still caught in Ginny's hair, but he started to lightly massage her neck. It had become a routine. Today he didn't feel any knots, so he lightened his touch to almost a caress. He knew he should stop, but he didn't seem to have the discipline to follow through. Finally, he withdrew his hand and felt like he had lost something.

"Pete," Ginny said, "do you have a significant other in Chicago?"

"No," he answered. "If I did, I would be moving heaven and earth to get to her. Do you have a significant other here?"

"No," she replied.

"Why not?" he asked.

"There never seemed to be time or opportunity," Ginny explained. "I was a skinny nerd in high school, so none of the boys asked me out. I was too busy in college. You have no idea how competitive it is to get into vet school. You need an almost perfect GPA plus hours of work in a clinic. Then there was the extra education and PhD. Then came the clinic. Then came the supplement business. So, there has always been something in the way. When I settled back here, any guy I knew before college was already married with two to four kids. So now I'm an old maid veterinarian. Why have you never married?"

"I worked after school in high school and to pay my way through college," Pete told her. "There was no time to date. Then I was in the army, then the Chicago police department, then I started my own business. I probably could have made the time and found a wife in college, but I knew I wanted to go into the army. It didn't seem fair to marry then leave. When I came back, I had such odd hours with the department that it was difficult to meet women. I mean, I met plenty of women, but no one I wanted to get to know well enough to marry. So now I am an old bachelor security expert."

"We're a pair, aren't we?" Ginny asked with a giggle that made Pete laugh, too.

"I guess we are," Pete said with a chuckle, "but truthfully, Ginny, I'm glad I met you. You have no idea how special you are."

"Aw, thank you, Pete," she said, looking at him. "You're pretty special yourself. You make me feel safe, but you also make me feel valued. I appreciate that."

"You're welcome." Pete said then thought, *that was a very personal conversation, and there was no awkwardness. This was a good sign.*

An hour later, Michael and Leah were making breakfast. The other adults were slowly gathering in the den. Suddenly, Ginny's phone rang.

"Woops," she said, "here we go. This is Dr. Reed." The men listened to her side of the conversation.

"How many were there? Anyone you know?" Ginny listened then asked, "Can you have Brady send me the pictures so we can take a look? Thanks." Ginny ended the call and turned to the group waiting for information.

"Tom Sutton has pictures of men entering his pasture last night," she said. "According to the time stamp they entered at 1:30 am, walked around and left at 1:45 am. Here come the pictures."

Ginny zoomed in on the figures in the picture as the men leaned over her shoulders for a better view.

"Know anybody?" Mark asked.

"Yes," Ginny said. "I hate it, but I recognize the one in front. That's Dwight Hall. He's a sheriff's deputy and has a wife and two kids. They're probably hungry. He's not a planner. Now we know why a deputy never responded to the Miller's complaint. Tom recognized him too."

"Do you think the sheriff knows?" Mark asked.

"I have no way of knowing," Ginny said. "Dwight was behind me in school. Brad may know him better."

"Brad may know what?" Brad asked, walking up to the group.

"Tom Sutton sent me a picture of the men who were walking through his pasture last night." Ginny said and held her phone up for Brad to see.

"Dwight Hall? He did that?" Brad exclaimed.

"Well, we know he was trying to do that last night," Mark said, and he looked at the computer watch schedule. "Bennett was on the computer during that time."

"They must not have driven by here, then," Pete said. "Bennett would have told me when I came on duty."

"Dwight was never the brightest star in the sky," Brad said, "but he would know where the cows were. He could always talk somebody into doing the carving to share the meat."

"Do you know him well enough to talk to him?" Mark asked.

"Not really, not enough to call him up and say, hey buddy, you were seen in a pasture," Brad said. "But if I ran into him, I could tell him about the thefts and see how he reacted. Unfortunately, we aren't going anywhere to run into anybody."

Garrett listened to the conversation then called Brett over.

"Brett, is there any way you could use the equipment you have to monitor the air and tell if a drone goes overhead?" Garrett asked.

"Maybe," Brett answered. "I'd have to research it and see if I can do it with my drone console or an app of some sort. The internet tends to be available as long as the power is on, so there might be something to download."

"Ok," Garret said. "That's your priority job this morning. Also, will you put the drone you brought in the air and count all the cows?"

"Sure," Brett said and went downstairs to get his drone.

"What are you thinking, Garrett?" Mark asked.

"Nobody can see your cows from the road," Garrett said, looking at Ginny and Brad. "However, if people know you have them, they may search for them from the air with drones. If the cows are in any way accessible, the thieves may strike again."

Leah announced that breakfast was ready. Pajama-clad children ran up the stairs and jumped in line to get food while the adults were leisurely moving to the kitchen island. When Aaron and Donna came through the back door, Ginny took her phone over and showed Aaron the pictures.

"What are we supposed to do now?" Aaron asked in a disgusted voice. "The very people we need to call on to help us are taking advantage of us."

"I don't know, Aaron," she said. "Garrett's worried someone may send drones to find our livestock."

"Well, that's just great. What else is going to happen?" he asked.

"We don't know," Ginny replied. "I can tell you what the Reed family does."

"What?" Aaron asked in an abrupt, disgusted voice.

"We pray, Aaron," Ginny stated. "We pray the farm. We hold hands and thank God for our blessings. Then we pray for forgiveness, guidance, and protection. It's a marvelous stress reliever, Aaron."

"You're right, Ginny," Aaron said. "I need to calm down and remember that. Thank you."

Ginny gave him a quick side hug. "You're welcome."

CHAPTER 27
APRIL 20

Just as everyone had started eating breakfast, Grace called out from the computers, "There's a car coming up the drive."

Mark, Pete, Alex, Brad, and Bennett ran to their rooms to grab firearms then took strategic posts in the house where they could look out windows onto the front yard. The car stopped at the front porch. Mark watched from the door.

A man got out of the driver's side. He was tall and lean, but his shirt was covered with blood, and his hands were shaking.

"Is the Doc here?" he called.

Mark locked his pistol and slid it into the holster on the back of his belt and leaned his rifle against the wall at the front door. Then he opened the door and stepped out onto the porch.

"Who are you and why do you need the doc?" Mark asked. "You could have called. She's in the phone book."

"We live down the road, and we didn't have time," the man said and pointed to the back seat. "We have a man who's been shot."

"Why didn't you take him to the hospital in Elkin?" Mark asked as he heard Ginny giving orders in the parlor. He knew she was going to help them.

"We couldn't get an ambulance. Please, help him," the man pleaded as he ran a shaky hand through his hair. "He's your neighbor, Daniel Speaks."

"Who shot him?" Mark asked.

"The scumbags trying to steal our cows," was the response.

"Bring him in!" Ginny called from the door.

The driver opened the door to the back seat. He and a second man helped their friend out of the car. Daniel cried out in pain, and his friends practically carried him inside.

"To the parlor," Ginny ordered. A portable table had been set up with a plastic drape across it and another spread out under it. Adam came running in with Ginny's tool kit.

"Where's he hit?" she asked.

"Left shoulder," a man answered as he helped Daniel lay down on the table. Ginny looked at the pale face of her friend and neighbor and almost cried.

"Daniel," Ginny said firmly, lightly tapping his cheek. "Daniel Speaks, open your eyes."

The man on the table opened his eyes and looked at Ginny. She could tell by the clench of his jaw that he was in pain.

"I'm going to take your shirt off, Daniel. That's all." Ginny said and used scissors to cut through the fabric.

Ginny held out a 4x4 gauze, and Erica poured saline on it. She used it to clean blood away from the wound then examined it.

"Daniel, I need to turn you over." Ginny looked at Erica, "Help me turn him. Just on his right side so I can see the exit wound."

Daniel cried out in pain when they moved him. Ginny peeled the remnants of the shirt from over the wound. Taking another piece of wet gauze, she cleaned around the wound.

Looking around, she said to Pete, "On the bookshelf in the den is a Gray's Anatomy. Bring it here and find the images of the musculature around the shoulder, scapula, and clavicle for me."

Pete left the room and came back quickly flipping through the pages, searching for what she needed. He held the book for Ginny, and she looked at the drawings as she probed the wound with her fingers.

"Adam, get that blue suture set, the bottle of lidocaine, and a syringe with a small needle." Ginny ordered. Erica continued to pour saline over the wound so Ginny could wipe it clean with sterile gauze. The bleeding had stopped.

"Daniel, you're lucky," she said. "The bullet went completely through. I don't have to look for it. The bleeding has stopped, which means it didn't hit a major artery or vein." Ginny filled the syringe with lidocaine and numbed the wound.

"Adam, open the sutures like I showed you in the clinic that time without touching what's inside." Adam did as she directed, and Ginny took the suture needle and thread.

"Daniel, I'm sorry, but this will still hurt." Ginny said and had Erica hold the muscles in place, and she began to suture them. Daniel cried out. Ginny stopped, giving the lidocaine more time to numb the area.

Finally, Ginny finished closing the wound on Daniel's back, bandaged it and turned him so she could examine the entry wound. She cleaned it with saline and used lidocaine to numb the area.

"This will hurt again," she said. The clavicle was bent and uneven, indicating that it was broken. She pressed gently and set the bones back in place, sutured the muscles and closed the wound. Ginny cleaned the skin and placed a bandage over the sutures.

"Brad, look in the first aid kit in the office; there should be material to use as a sling," Ginny said.

When Brad returned, Ginny had Daniel's friends help him sit up. She put the sling over his right shoulder and secured his left arm to his chest.

Ginny looked at Daniel's friends, "Do you have a blanket or large towel in the car?"

"Yes, Ma'am," the driver answered. "I keep one in there."

"Would you bring it in?" Ginny asked. When he brought the blanket back, Ginny wrapped it around Daniel, being careful to not get it in any saline or blood that was still on the table.

"How do you know Daniel?" she asked the man.

"I'm Blake Stevens; I'm married to his sister," he said. "We live in Winston, and he's letting us stay with him."

"What happened?" she asked.

"It was barely daylight," Blake said. "Daniel saw two men on the road crossing over into his pasture. They were trying to corner a young steer. Daniel grabbed his shotgun and went out to confront them. He yelled at them to stop, and one aimed a pistol at him and fired. Doc, he hadn't even raised the shotgun. When Daniel fell, the two men ran out of the pasture and down the road. I called 911, but they told me the ambulance service was no longer working and the sheriff was out on a call. Daniel said you could help him."

Ginny looked at Daniel and asked, "Do you know who shot you?"

Daniel got a fearful look on his face and nodded yes.

"Do *I* know who shot you?" she asked. Daniel nodded yes.

"Do you want to tell me who it was?" she asked.

"It was Dwight Hall," Daniel whispered to Ginny.

Ginny spoke back softly, "I thought so. We're pretty sure he's responsible for all the cattle deaths around here. No one will know you said anything, but you know I have to report this."

Daniel's eyes grew wide and fearful. "Please don't, Ginny," he whispered. "He'll retaliate against my family. Dwight's like that."

"All right," Ginny said. "I'll wait until you're ready." She turned back to the other men.

"Blake, who else is at the house with you?" she asked.

"My wife, our two kids, Janie, and Mason, our cousin," Blake said and pointed to the man with him. "We expect Daniel's brother any time. He's trying to get here from Richmond."

"Daniel, I want you to come to my clinic tomorrow morning," Ginny said, looking back at her neighbor. "I will meet you there at ten. I want to check your bandage."

Ginny turned to his family members. "Blake, can you get him there?"

"Yes, Ma'am," Blake answered.

"Hold him steady," Ginny said to Erica. "I'll be right back."

Ginny went into the office and came out with two pain pills and a glass of water. She helped Daniel take the medication then gave another set of pills and instructions to Blake.

"I'll check him in the morning, but call me if you have any questions," Ginny told Blake. "Daniel has my number. Okay, let's walk him to your car."

Ginny helped Blake and Mason put Daniel in the car.

"Drive easy, Blake." Ginny said. "When you get home, wrap some ice in plastic and a towel. Then gently hold it in place it over both wounds for ten minutes, no longer. It will help with the swelling and pain."

"Thank you, Doc," Daniel said in a weak voice that was laced with pain. He held his right hand out to her. "I don't know what I would have done without your help. How can I repay you?"

"Get well." Ginny whispered as she took his hand in hers, "and bring me some of that brandy you make every summer."

"I'll do that," Daniel said with a grin and a grimace.

Ginny closed the car door then climbed the porch steps and sat heavily in one of the wicker chairs. Garrett sat beside her and gave her a glass of ice water. Ginny's hands were trembling when she took it.

"You did good, Ginny," he said.

"Garrett, I'm not a medical doctor," she answered, sounding miserable. "I could lose my license for what I just did."

"You had no choice under the circumstances," Garrett said softly. "The usual path for humans to get medical help was closed to him.

You'll be covered under a law that prevents people who step up to help from being sued."

"I don't want word to get around that I will treat people," Ginny said, "but I'm afraid it will. What do I do then?"

"This was an emergency, Ginny. Anything else, you send them to Elkin," he answered calmly.

"That makes sense," Ginny said, nodding.

Mark came over, "You okay, Ginny?"

"Yes," Ginny answered. "We need to rethink the driveway, though. Put a wire fence across it just inside the trees, then on this side of the wire put the rebar. Anyone wanting help would probably stop at the fence. Anyone going through the fence deserves to have his tires blown, but I would have felt terrible if that man had lost his tires over this." She paused. "I need to clean the parlor."

"It's done," Garrett said. "Adam helped Erica take care of it. Did you know he wants to be a veterinarian like you?"

"I thought maybe he did," Ginny said, smiling. "He was full of questions when ya'll were here over Christmas, and I let him go to the clinic with me. He'll be good. Maybe I should let him go with me on the next call, if I go out on any more calls. Those may be over."

Ginny stood up and walked into the house. Everyone was standing around the television.

"What happened?" Ginny asked.

"Well," Mark said, "first the government isn't going to put any more money on the food stamp accounts or other government assistance programs. Social security checks will be withheld in May. They said all funds are being diverted to the military and recovery efforts. I think the government is broke."

"And second?" Ginny asked.

Mark continued, "China has announced it is now officially North Korea's ally. Any country who fires more bombs at them will be met with the full force of the Chinese army. Russia is attacking and moving further into Ukraine. NATO is whining about that but not doing anything. I think the Europeans are hoping to stay out of this. Even our own allies are distant.

"A few more obscure terrorist groups have taken credit for bombing our cities. The military doesn't know who to target. They finally announced that the material in the bombs has been traced to Iran, Russia, China, and believe it or not, Brazil and South Africa. It looks like a cooperative operation."

Pete looked over at Bennett, who looked back. Pete gave him a nod of respect for having that information several days ago.

"The military is on high alert," Mark continued. "The CIA, FBI, and Secret Service are working together to find out if any more American sites are being targeted. There you have it."

"Better make the garden bigger," Ginny said to Brad who was standing beside her.

Everyone dispersed to start their chores for the day. Ginny took her hair down and fixed her ponytail. Pete noticed her hands were still trembling. He went to the refrigerator and got one of the last carbonated beverages full of sugar. Taking Ginny's hand, he led her to the porch swing, opened the drink and handed it to her.

"You're coming down from an adrenaline rush," Pete said. "Drink this. It will give you a sugar boost at least."

"Thank you." She took a sip of the beverage, smiled, and sighed. "I'm going to miss these when they're all gone. It isn't the taste; it's all about the bubbles."

Pete smiled, leaned back into the swing and put his arm on the back of it. Ginny leaned against him while she slowly sipped the drink. Pete gently moved the swing back and forth.

Ginny sighed, "Pete, why is it you always know how to calm my anxiety and soothe my nerves? How do you do that?"

"I don't know, Ginny," he answered. "It's like I see you and notice everything about you. Why is that?"

"I don't know, Pete," she said. "Maybe we were meant to be great friends."

"Maybe so." Pete continued to rock the swing and talk with Ginny. Eventually her hands stopped trembling and she laughed at his corny jokes.

"Will you be all right, now?" he asked.

"Yes. I'm fine, thank you," Ginny said. "Aren't you are supposed to be checking game cameras?"

"Yes, but Alex is waiting until you're feeling better," Pete replied.

"Don't keep him waiting any longer on my account," Ginny said, making a moving motion with her hands. "Go. Shoo."

Pete laughed and stood up. He turned back and reached his hand out to Ginny to help her out of the swing. She took it and started to stand, but the swing moved and she lost her balance. Pete caught her just as she was about to fall. The embrace caught them both by surprise. Their eyes locked. Ginny stared at Pete, and he stared back at her.

"Close call," Pete said, snapping back to reality. "We can't have our very own resident Doc getting hurt."

"I guess not," she replied. The two went into the house, but Ginny couldn't stop thinking about that embrace.

Pete and Alex took the four-wheeler to check the cameras. As hard as he tried to concentrate on the work, Pete could not get the embrace with Ginny out of his mind.

Several of the men were securing the driveways for both farms. Brad was on the tractor tilling the garden plot and extending it into one of the fields. The children were having classes in the basement. Grace and Ceely started prepping lunch, and Barbara was starting laundry.

Ginny searched for Erica. She found her in the basement looking for laundry detergent to help Barbara.

"Erica," she said."

"Yes?" Erica asked.

"I guess we need to go over medical plans," Ginny said. "I never dreamed we would have to resort to what we did this morning. It happened so fast. Adam was there assisting, but I think next time it should be you, and he can hold the patient still. He's eager to help, but he has no concept of infection control."

"Okay. What do you want to do?" Erica asked.

"Let's go upstairs," Ginny said. "You can hand that detergent off to Barbara, and then I want you to show me the inventory of medical supplies."

Ginny and Erica sat at the dining room table while Ginny looked at the list.

"These supplies are in the house, correct?" Ginny asked.

"Yes," Erica answered.

"We need to inventory what's in my trailer and the equipment shed," Ginny said. "I don't keep much bandage size gauze, just what I need to clean wounds and stop bleeding. I'm also low on sterile gloves. So, let's put those items on a wish list."

The two women spent the rest of the morning recording supplies that had come from the clinic and made a list of what they felt they would need if they had to treat people instead of animals. They placed supplies in the parlor in case there was a repeat of the morning's emergency.

"I'm going to the clinic in the morning to recheck Daniel's bandages. Will you come, too?" Ginny asked Erica. "We can set up the surgical area for people, just in case. Also, I want you to look at the wound. I know signs of infection in animals, but as a nurse, you may recognize it quicker on a person. Shoot, I forgot to ask Daniel if he was allergic to any meds. I'll take a couple different kinds of antibiotics with me. I need to read up on what to give humans."

Looking at the clock, the two women gathered with the others for lunch. Before getting food, Ginny approached Ceely.

"Ceely, will you come to the clinic with me tomorrow morning?" she asked. "I'm going to check Daniel's bandages, but I want you to look at the shoulder. The clavicle is broken and needs to heal, but since you're a physical therapist, I want you to see if he needs any exercises to keep the shoulder working."

"Sure. I'll be glad to. You did well this morning. I just wanted you to know that," Ceely said.

"Thanks," Ginny replied. "I hope I don't have to do that on another human while this crisis is going on. I had planned to help my family if I could, but I don't want the responsibility of trying to keep a community of people healthy. That's not my knowledge base. Besides, if word got out, I could lose my license or go to jail."

"Don't worry," Ceely said, patting Ginny on the back. "I'm sure Garrett knows those legalities and could help you out, but I somehow believe that Daniel is not going to complain."

"I hope not," Ginny replied.

Chapter 28

April 20

During lunch, Adam discreetly showed Barbara the news banner on his phone. Barbara looked over at the younger children who had finished eating.

"Donna," she said, "would you and Grace mind if I send the children downstairs with Bonnie and Hannah?"

The women agreed. When the older girls had the younger children downstairs playing games, Barbara turned on the television.

"I think we want to see what's happening," she said. The adults moved so they could see the television, curious as to what they might learn.

The news reported riots taking place all over the country. People were in an angry panic and protesting the plan to not fund the government assistance programs or social security, but they were angrier that food was in short supply. People were angry that the government had not kept them safe from terrorist attacks and that they were now being forced into their homes by martial law.

Vandalism was rampant in the large cities with people fighting over supplies. Fire departments and emergency medical services were overwhelmed with calls and understaffed because workers were staying home to take care of their families. People were afraid of more terrorist attacks and were fleeing the cities only to be stranded on the highways because the gas stations had not been resupplied.

"What an absolute nightmare," Barbara said. "Those poor people on the roads."

"I don't think we'll be immune from this," Mark said. "People around here are also on government assistance for a lot of different reasons. I'm sure they're worried about losing the funds for a month, too. They just aren't rioting." Mark paused then said, "It's not just people on government assistance. None of us are working right now. By next month we'll all feel the pinch of no income." The group was quiet as they continued to watch the drama play out on the screen.

"Brett," Garrett said and motioned to his son, "were you able to establish a system for detecting drones?"

"Sort of," he replied. "I found this in the attic." He held up a microphone.

"That was mine!" Garrett exclaimed, laughing. "It's an old Mr. Microphone."

"I took it apart," Brett said, holding up the device, "and instead of projecting a voice, it detects other sounds. I sync'd a computer program with the transistors so that it will only collect a particular sound, a drone. I can put this on a rooftop, and it should detect the sound of any drone within about a quarter of a mile. Sorry, I couldn't do any better with what I could find."

Everyone started clapping.

"Do better? Son, you're remarkable," Garret said. "Let's go to the barn and see if we can set it up."

"Dad," Brett said as they were walking to the barn, "I don't mean to sound snobbish, but do you really think the people this far out in the country will have drones?"

"Brett, you have no idea," Garrett said laughing. "A lot of the farmers around here have college degrees in agriculture. They use drones to check their crops and livestock all the time. Now that I think about it, I don't know if Brad has one, but I think Mr. Johnson does."

"You can go to college to learn agriculture?" Brett asked.

"Sure," Garrett said. "There are two universities that have those programs in our state, and there are programs at several community colleges."

"I'll tell Michael," Brett said. "He's become fascinated by the farm, but he's too shy to ask Brad to show him anything."

"I'll tell Brad that Michael has an interest. Maybe he can get Michael to talk to him about it," Garrett replied.

Garrett and Brett climbed into the hay loft. At a large opening at one end of the loft, Garrett looped a rope over the pulley that was formerly used to lift straw and hay bales through the opening. Then he tied the microphone in the middle of the rope and lifted it to the height of the pulley. The other end of the rope could be used to bring the microphone back down.

"How's the reception," Garret asked.

Brett looked at his tablet. "Good. It's a clear day, so that helps."

"Any signals?" Garrett asked.

"No," Brett replied, "but from the loft I can monitor the reception and occasionally send my drone out over the farm." Brett looked out the loft opening. "Wow. You can really see a lot from up here. Is that a creek?"

"Yes. Have I never taken you there?" Garrett asked.

"Maybe," Brett said, "but I must have been too little to remember it. I know I've never seen it from up here."

"We'll have to make a trip one Sunday," Garrett said and pulled the microphone back into the barn. "Let's go back to the house. We know we can get reception from here. We just need to make a plan on how to use this."

Garrett and Brett walked back to the house to let everyone know that the microphone could get reception and that everything was quiet. While they were standing in the kitchen, Brett's microphone started to beep and make a humming noise.

"It works! And we're inside!" Brett exclaimed in surprise and ran outside.

Garrett grabbed the set of binoculars he had taken to the barn and joined Brett.

"Can you tell where it is?" Garrett asked.

"Not well, I think it's coming from the north," Brett said.

Garrett took the binoculars and scanned the sky. He stopped when he saw a dark spot hovering over the Sutton farm. He focused the binoculars and saw that it was a drone flying side to side in a grid pattern over the pastures. While he was watching, the drone flared so brightly that Garrett moved the binoculars away from his eyes. When he looked through them again, the sky was empty, but there was a small tendril of smoke rising from the pasture grass.

"What happened?" he asked. "I think it exploded."

"I think Bennett happened," Mark said, standing at Garrett's side, and pointing to the barn loft. He could just barely see a man in the shadows on the floor of the loft. A few minutes later Bennett walked out of the barn and went to his truck.

Mark joined him as he was opening the truck door to put his rifle on the passenger's seat.

"Nice shooting," Mark said. "How did you know to look for a drone?"

"Thanks," Bennett replied. "I met Tom Sutton the other day when I was walking around the farm. We talked across the fence. Nice guy. I know he doesn't have a drone because I asked him. It just made sense that someone would use that technology to find cows that were no longer near the road. They would need to use it in the daytime, and I figured there had been enough time for whoever is doing this to get a drone in the air. As soon as I heard Brett's alarm, I got my rifle and ran to the barn. That drone was definitely looking for his cows. I didn't want it to get any closer to this place."

"You had sniper training, didn't you?" Mark asked.

Bennett paused then said, "Yes."

Mark nodded in understanding and asked no more questions.

Clouds moved across the sky and by dinner a light mist was falling. After the meal Pete asked Ginny to join him on the front porch. A couple of the parents were in the basement watching a movie with the kids while the rest were playing a large game of rummy at the dining room table.

Ginny sat down in the swing and Pete sat beside her. He put his arm across the back of the swing. Ginny leaned in against him and placed her head on his shoulder.

"When I was a kid, I loved to sit out here and read when it was raining," Ginny said. "Well, in the summertime, that is. Too cold in the winter."

"I bet so," Pete said, smiling.

"Pete, what will you do when all this is over?" she asked.

"I don't know," Pete said. "I may try to salvage what I can from Chicago, although I will just leave it if it's radioactive. I have no idea where my employees are, who's still working, who have left their posts, or who may be dead. I imagine they're all taking care of their families because most aren't responding to my texts for information. I wish I had a few of them here. Maybe I'll just stay here and become a farmer and veterinarian's assistant."

"Don't tease me now," Ginny said seriously. "I would love that."

Pete stilled the swing and looked at her. "Would you?"

Ginny looked at him and said, "Yes."

Pete looked at her for a moment then leaned in and gently kissed her lips. It was gentle, sweet, and the best kiss he ever had. Ginny placed her hand on his cheek when she felt him start to pull away and kissed him back.

Ginny slid closer to Pete, pulled his arm tighter around her and sighed, "I liked that, Peter Flinn. I could get used to it."

"I liked it too Ginny Reed," Pete said and started to move the swing again. He looked out across the evening sky. "I would like very much to get used to it."

The movie watchers and rummy players had all gone to their rooms when Mark went to lock the front door. He heard laughter on the porch. He started to open the door then realized it was Ginny and Pete. He turned and went upstairs, smiling to himself. They could lock up.

CHAPTER 29
APRIL 21

Ginny entered the kitchen before sunrise. Looking into the den, she saw Bennett sitting at the computer.

"Is everything quiet?" she asked.

"Yep," he replied.

"Good," she said. "I'm going to turn on the television. I had a news banner on my phone about Russia and Ukraine."

Ginny turned the television to the national news.

"What happened?" Bennett asked.

"Russia has conquered Ukraine," Ginny said. "The US and NATO had been supplying Ukraine with weapons, but that seems to have stopped. The ousted Ukrainian government is appealing to the United Nations for help, NATO is blustering, and the US is quiet on the subject. Iran, Iraq, and Turkey have allied against Israel. China has taken Taiwan. Japan is still complaining to the UN about the island dispute with China. And the President, along with the Federal Reserve, has declared a bank holiday. They say it's to save the economy, but all banks in the US are closed today. There must have been too many people wanting their money at the same time. And there you have it, for now."

"No one has to invade us," Bennett said as he kept his eyes on the computer screen. "We're imploding from within." Bennett paused, "Ginny, will you go wake Brad."

"Sure, is something wrong?" she asked.

"Not sure," Bennett said, frowning.

Ginny knocked on Brad's door and gave him Bennett's message. Brad came out of the office trying to shake the sleep from his head.

"Whatcha got, Bennett?" Brad asked.

Bennett pointed to the image on the screen of the house Brad now owned. There were two people in the driveway facing the house and pointing at it.

"I'm going over there," Brad said.

"Not without me," Bennett

replied.

"Or me." Pete came into the kitchen.

"I'll watch the screens," Ginny said.

Brad holstered a pistol and draped a pump action shot gun over his back as he walked out of the house. Starting the four-wheeler, he took the trail across the farm to the house he now owned. Bennett and Pete followed in Bennett's truck. They accessed the road through the gate behind Ginny's animal clinic.

Ginny continued to watch the monitors. Brad stopped the four-wheeler in front of the two people before they got all the way to the house and was confronting them. They appeared to be arguing. Eventually the two people left, heading south until they were out of camera range.

Ginny checked her phone for the feed from the cameras she had at the clinic. They walked past the parking lot but didn't bother the building; they kept walking south. Back on the computer screen, she saw Brad, Pete, and Bennett talking in the yard of the house. Brad went into the house while Pete and Bennett left in the truck.

A few minutes later Pete and Bennett came in through the back door.

"What happened?" she asked.

"It was some of the Smith family," Pete answered. "It seems they've run out of space at their place and wanted to use Brad's. They hadn't planned to ask because they thought the Thompsons still owned it and had abandoned it. One of the men got angry because it's sitting empty, and they needed the room. Brad still wouldn't let them use it, and I don't blame him. After all this is over, anyone still in it could possibly claim squatter's rights. Brad wants to use some of the plywood to board it up like we did Aaron's house."

The group heard footsteps on the stairs. They turned and saw Mark walk into the den.

"Something happen?" he asked. Pete told him what had taken place.

"We may not have enough plywood," Mark said, "but we could put one-by-fours across the upstairs windows. Where's Brad?"

"He stayed at the house," Bennett replied. "We promised to take him some food and coffee, and then show up with the plywood and Mike's ladders."

"What about Mike's ladders?" Mike asked as he came into the kitchen. "I heard the truck and four-wheeler leave across the pasture. What happened?"

Pete gave him an abbreviated version of the incident and the need to put plywood over the windows and doors of Brad's house.

"I can help with that," Mike said. "Is there any more coffee?"

Bennett returned to the computers, and Ginny started making another pot of coffee.

"I guess it's a good thing I bought so much of this stuff," she said, grinning as she measured grounds into the filter. "I also brought the supply over from the clinic. You guys drink as much as I do."

Ginny looked at the menu and started to prep breakfast. It wasn't her day to cook, but she thought she would get things started. They were going to have a busy morning.

By mid-morning, the house was quiet. The kids were having lessons, including the high school and middle school students. Most of the adults were outside working on the farms or at Brad's house.

Ceely and Erica got into Ginny's work truck, and Ginny drove through the farm to the clinic to meet Daniel Speaks. His sutures looked good with no signs of infection. Ceely showed him some mild exercises to keep the shoulder moving but would not hurt the clavicle. Ginny sent Daniel on his way with antibiotics, instructions to call if infection started and to call in a week for another check. After the men were gone, they cleaned the surgical area and left it ready in case of another emergency.

Back at the house, Ginny turned on the television. The national news showed continued riots in the cities. Stores were boarded up, people were spray painting grafitti on the walls of buildings, and government offices were being vandalized over the loss of assistance programs. It showed lines at ATM machines which allowed depositors to get only $200 a day. Roads were still blocked with disabled vehicles, and then it showed video clips of what the commentators were calling a crisis phenomenon.

In the videos, large groups of people were banding together and walking out of the cities. As they traveled, the people who were stranded on the road joined them. One reporter had joined the back of a group. He described the group members as angry and willing to do whatever they needed to survive. He showed the devastation the group left behind. Homes and businesses were gutted by fire. A community garden had been stripped bare. Any deer that had been unfortunate to be too close was killed and cooked. What concerned Ginny most were the videos of what appeared to be a farm, completely engulfed in flames. All the buildings were gone, and gardens were stripped bare of cool season plants.

Ginny switched to the Winston Salem channel to check the local news. They carried the same news the national stations had. A local reporter followed a large group of people leaving Greensboro and traveling north. One of the members of the group said they couldn't find food in Greensboro, and the streets had become unsafe, so they were going to rural Virginia and the mountains. Ginny turned the television off. She paused for a moment then called Mark.

"Hey. Is something wrong?" he asked.

"How long before you're finished boarding up Brad's house?" Ginny asked him.

"Not long, why?" he asked.

"No emergency, but I saw a report on the television we need to discuss," Ginny said. "Also, we wanted to know if you were going to be back for lunch or if you wanted us to save something for you."

"We're about to finish here," Mark said. "We should be back in time for lunch."

"Okay. See you in a bit." Ginny went to tell Leah she wouldn't have to save any food for the men who were working at Brad's house.

After lunch, Ginny told the other adults about the report of large groups of people walking out of the cities. Most were traveling to rural areas or the mountains thinking they could survive off the land.

"My concern," Ginny said, "is what if people leave Winston or Charlotte and come through here. A crowd could take everything we have. How do we prepare for that?"

"We will have to rely on God to protect us from that," Garrett said. "There's no other way."

"I agree," Mark said. "But we need to plan as well. Any ideas?"

"I found some tall game fencing in Mr. Thompson's barn," Brad said. "I was going to put it around the garden, but I think there's enough to expand it to also enclose the area between the buildings. It won't stop a determined group, but it'll keep the lone thief out. Also,

I've been worried about dogs left to fend for themselves. That fence will allow the little kids to play outside without having an armed adult nearby watching for dogs or coyotes."

"Good idea. We'll start that today. Any other ideas?" Mark asked.

"The barn where we're living has a root cellar under it," Aaron said. "We can go ahead and put some supplies there. If we think a hoard is coming, we can always take some more out there."

"Two good ideas," Mark said. "Let's get the fencing over here today. Then we'll decide the perimeter to enclose."

Brett's microphone started buzzing. Everyone went outside to see if they could spot the drone. Bennett took his rifle to the barn loft.

"I see it," Garrett said looking through his binoculars. "It has just crossed the Sutton farm and is over our pastures." The group heard a gunshot, and Garrett jerked the binoculars away from his eyes. When he looked again it was gone.

"Well, it just exploded," Garrett said. "Way to go, Bennett."

"Was it close enough to see our pastures?" Mark asked.

"Possibly. It depends on the range of the cameras," Garrett said.

A few minutes later, Bennett came out of the barn, his rifle slung across his back. He approached the group standing in the backyard.

"It found the cows, no question. I could tell from the rifle scope." Bennett looked at Mark, "Can you replace Pete and me on the computers tonight?"

"Yes. Going huntin'?" Mark asked.

Bennett looked at Pete then back to Mark, "Yep."

CHAPTER 30
APRIL 21

That night while everyone else got ready for bed, Bennett and Pete prepared to spend the night in the pasture. Pete slid a flashlight into his pocket. Bennett watched Pete then gestured to the pocket the flashlight had disappeared into.

"You may not need that. Here." Bennett handed Pete a headset with night vision.

"This is nice equipment," Pete said. "Where did you get it?"

"The main advantage of working at an outdoor store," Bennett said, smiling, "is the employee discount."

Pete laughed and followed Bennett out the door. Outside, away from the house, they put on the night vision goggles and adjusted the settings. Once they could see, they opened the pasture gate and went inside.

The two men walked about fifty acres before they found the cows clustered under some trees at the far end of the pasture. Pete and Bennett chose an observation point a short distance away on a slight hill and settled in for the night. Bennett watched the north and east while Pete watched the south and west. They waited patiently, sure they would catch the thieves. Then, at about one in the morning, they noticed two men approaching from the road, northwest of the cows.

"That is the closest route to the road," Bennett whispered. "I checked the farm's aerial maps this afternoon." Bennett shook his head, "The idiots are using flashlights. That's like a beacon saying here I am."

Pete and Bennett followed the tree line to get closer to the cows. They stopped at the south edge of the herd just as the men reached the north edge of the cows. One man culled a steer from the herd. They saw him raise his knife above the animal.

"I wouldn't do that if I were you," Bennett called out. "That steer doesn't belong to you."

The man froze, knife in his hand. The other man pulled a pistol from a holster.

"I wouldn't do *that* either," Pete said. "There's more than one gun pointing at you. Drop the weapon." The pistol fell to the ground.

"Turn off your flashlights," Bennett said.

The flashlights went out. Thanks to the night vision goggles, Pete saw one man trying to regain his gun.

"Freeze!" Pete shouted. "I didn't tell you to pick the weapon up." Pete could see the surprise on the man's face.

Bennett ordered loudly, "Move away from the cows and sit on the ground."

The men did as they were directed. Bennett took out his cell phone and called Mark.

"Yeah," Mark's groggy voice answered. "Did they come?" He received an affirmative reply. "Okay, I'll get Alex and Brad. Be there in ten minutes."

Ten minutes later they could see the lights on a truck and the four-wheeler coming down the farm paths from the house. Bennett and Pete turned off the night vision but kept their weapons aimed at the men.

Mark and Brad parked so that their lights shone on the two men who were still sitting on the ground. Alex stayed in the shadows, armed and watching, while Mark and Brad came around behind Pete and Bennett.

Mark asked Brad, "Do you know these two?"

"I know one," Brad said in a disgusted voice as he looked at the smaller of the two men who had his head down, looking at the ground.

"Dwight Hall," Brad said harshly, "what're you doing out here stealing cattle? You're supposed to be upholding the law, not breaking it."

"Brad, you don't understand," Dwight complained. "Our kids are hungry. You don't have kids. You got no idea what it's like to see your children cry with empty bellies."

"Who's with you, Dwight?" Brad asked.

"A neighbor," Dwight answered sullenly.

"Dwight, did you shoot Daniel Speaks?" Brad asked.

"I didn't mean to," Dwight said, his voice trembling. "I was just shooting in the air to scare him. Is he okay? He ain't dead, is he?"

"Does the sheriff know you're doing this?" Brad asked, deliberately choosing not to answer Dwight's question.

"No," Dwight said strongly. "He'd fire me. Sheriff's a good man, Brad. He wouldn't stand for this. He's trying hard to keep things running smooth in the county."

"That's good to hear," Mark mumbled.

"Where's your truck?" Brad asked.

"On the road, behind the trees."

"Give me your keys," Brad said.

"Aw, Brad, don't take mah truck!" Dwight whined.

"I'm not," Brad answered. "But you're going to walk home. I'll leave your truck at the end of the road tomorrow. Then you go to Elkin. We heard the Baptist church is collecting food, and they have a soup kitchen. Your family can eat one meal a day there. If there's any left over, maybe you can take some home."

Brad stepped closer to the deputy and leaned down.

"Dwight," he said firmly, "you better start planting a garden or find a way to barter for food instead of stealing it. This is going to last a long time, and you don't know how long money is going to be worth anything. You and your neighbors need to work together. Can you do that?"

"Maybe," Dwight answered sullenly.

"No maybe, Dwight," Brad insisted in a disgusted voice. "You have no choice if you want to survive. If you steal from the wrong farmer, you'll be dead, and your family will never know what happened to you. Do you understand?"

Dwight was quiet, but his friend said, "I understand. We ran out of food, and we don't have gardens. I told him this was stupid, but we were desperate. I didn't know about the church in Elkin." The man looked angrily at Dwight, "From here on out, if Dwight won't work to grow or trade for food, he won't eat."

"Dwight," Brad continued, "I won't tell the sheriff this time. But if I find out you're doing this again, I'll let him know. Where did you get the drones?"

"Another neighbor," Dwight quietly and sullenly. "We all shared the meat."

Brad whispered to Mark, "Move the four-wheeler so the lights point out to the road."

When Mark had done that, Brad said to the two men, "Okay. Go. I'll leave the truck at the end of the road sometime tomorrow. I'm not going to give you the chance to kill somebody else's cow tonight."

Dwight said nothing. He turned and walked away.

His friend stood and said, "Thank you. You could have shot us, but you didn't. I'll get the neighbors together and plant a community garden." Then he whispered, "Dwight's a lazy bum. I should've never listened to him, but like I said, we're desperate."

"If he starts this up again," Brad said, "call the sheriff. But whatever you do, you can't help him next time."

"I know." The man turned and walked away.

"Do you think Dwight will listen?" Mark asked.

"No. He's too lazy to be smart," Brad answered. "He's going to get killed, and then where will his kids be? Come on, let's go back. I'm tired." The men returned to the house.

CHAPTER 31

APRIL 23

Ginny came down the stairs at dawn. She walked over to the computer where Pete was sitting and kissed him on the cheek. Picking up his cup, she walked into the kitchen, refilled his coffee, and poured herself a cup.

"All quiet?" she asked.

"All quiet."

"According to the news from Winston Salem, it's supposed to rain soon" Ginny said as she placed Pete's now full coffee cup beside him. "I'm glad Robert and the teens got the garden planted. Hopefully, we will see baby plants in a week or so. I'm going to turn on the television." Ginny turned the television to a national news station.

Pete heard her sniffle.

"What is it?" he asked, not taking his eyes off the monitors.

"China has announced Taiwan's integration into the government of mainland China," Ginny said. "Russia continues to claim Ukraine is part of Russia and has placed troops along all the borders with eastern European countries. Iran has declared war on Israel. The terrorists hit us again. I don't know how many bombs they detonated, but they managed to hit power plants in New York and Pennsylvania, and petroleum refineries in Houston. More bombs were detonated in Manhattan, Atlanta, Chicago, San Francisco, Seattle, and Miami.

"The terrorists had large portable weapon launchers hidden on cargo ships still out on the ocean that they used to destroy the Port of Tacoma, the Port of Seattle, the Port of Savannah, and the Port of Norfolk. Also, they used speed boats and portable rocket launchers to blow up three bridges across the Mississippi River, at St. Louis, Memphis, and Baton Rouge. There are other bridges across the Mississippi, but the damaged ones are major interstates. This will make it harder to transport supplies by truck. I hope they don't destroy the others and cut the country completely in half.

"The same groups are taking credit. Some are even arguing over who is really responsible. It seems they all want the credit. This is from the news network in Atlanta. New York based companies are off the air because they were knocked offline by the bombs."

"Come here," Pete said. "I can't leave the computer."

"How are they getting away with this!" Ginny exclaimed angrily as she sat in the folding chair beside Pete. "Our government isn't doing anything!"

"We don't know how the government is responding," he said as he put his arm around her. He leaned his head against hers. "We will survive this."

Mark came down the stairs and looked over at Pete and Ginny. Pete had his arm around her, rubbing her shoulder. He saw Ginny's red eyes and heard her sniffling.

"What happened?" he asked.

"It's on the television. See for yourself," Ginny said, drying her tears.

People came down the stairs and in from the campers outside. Everyone gathered around the television. Grace, Hannah and Bonnie left the group to cook breakfast.

Normally, meals were full of conversation, but this morning everyone was quiet while they ate, trying to process what they had seen on the television. The only sounds were forks scraping plates and the occasional slurp of coffee. Garrett was getting ready to speak when the lights went out and the television screen went dark. A few seconds later, the generator started and electricity was restored, but Ginny stood and started giving orders.

"Everyone take a room," she said as she opened the blinds on the window in the dining room. "Switch off all the lights and unplug everything but the computers, refrigerator and freezer. We need to conserve fuel for the generator."

Ginny took the parlor, hallways, mudroom and laundry room. Then she went from room to room checking behind everyone. When that was done everyone regathered in the dining room.

"I guess this is it," Mark said. "We knew this was likely to happen, but I was just hoping I was wrong. Let's go to the backyard. I want Garrett to pray for us all. Then we need to build a fence."

The day's priority was building the fence. A strand of barbed wire fencing was placed in a shallow trench where the fence was to go. Then Brad used the tractor to dig the post holes. Alex and Pete inserted the posts while Adam, Brett, and Michael filled dirt in around the them. Mark, Garrett, and Bennett stretched the fencing and attached it to the posts. As the day progressed, everyone grew tired and irritable. They were hot and dirty, and there was no chance for a hot shower. The outdoor shower was completed, but it would not have hot, continuous water to wash off caked dirt or soothe achy muscles.

While the fence was being built, Ginny took the lids off all the toilet tanks. She filled several two gallon buckets with water from the hand pump in the backyard and placed them in each bathroom for flushing. She also left buckets of water at the steps of the RVs. Checking the toilet paper in the outhouse, she added several more rolls.

Erica and Holly put every available portable table in the back yard. Candles were placed in the kitchen and dining room. Oil lamps were put in the adult bedrooms. Battery operated lanterns were placed in the bathrooms and in the basement for the children.

A subdued group assembled outside for supper. The menu had been substituted with hotdogs and hamburgers cooked on the grill. While they sat at the portable tables eating, the generator stopped running and the back porch light came on. Everyone cheered.

Ginny stood and said, "If you worked on the fence go shower now in case this doesn't last long. Everybody, charge your electrical devices. When the men are out of the bathroom, if anyone else wants to bathe or shower do it now. Everyone was running around trying to get everything done as quickly as possible. Ginny and Holly took the food inside. Then they came back for the tables and chairs.

Ginny was working in the kitchen when Bonnie and Hannah came in. "Miss Ginny?"

"Yes, Bonnie?"

"May we use the shower in your room?"

"Yes, go ahead," Ginny answered.

Pete came out of his bathroom wearing gym shorts and a t-shirt. "My shower is free if anyone wants it," he called upstairs.

"I do," Mark yelled back and came down the stairs. "Can I use soap and shampoo? Mine are in the bathroom upstairs and Alex is in there."

"Sure. Use whatever you need, just not the toothbrush," Pete answered.

"No problem, there. Thanks"

Pete looked around and realized he and Ginny were alone in the kitchen. He hugged Ginny from behind and kissed her on the cheek.

"Are you going to shower?" he asked.

"Yes, after everyone has finished." She answered. "I didn't get as hot and dirty as most of you did."

When Brett came up the stairs from the basement, Ginny said,

"Brett, would you take your mother's spot at the computer so she can get a shower?"

"Sure. Mom, go. I got this."

"Thanks, Brett," Barbara said as she hurried up the stairs.

Adam came into the kitchen.

"Adam," Ginny said. "Will you see if you can find any information about the power outage. Our power comes from a co-op called Foothill Electric, but I have no idea where they get their power. Royal Energy is to the south and covers most of that area."

"Sure," he said. "I'll see what I can find out for you."

Ginny turned and saw Pete watching her.

"What?" she asked. "Something on my face?"

"No. I was just noticing that while you give Mark all the credit for running this place, he has nothing on you. You have organized emergency showers for everyone and put everything in place if the power goes out again. You give yourself too little credit."

"That's sweet, Pete. Thank you. It's nice to be noticed," Ginny said smiling.

Pete whispered, "Honey, I notice everything about you."

"I think I like that," Ginny replied with a grin.

Ginny set the leftover hamburgers and hotdogs from supper on the kitchen island for anyone who had not gotten enough to eat. She turned as Holly bounced downstairs and into the kitchen with wet hair and in clean clothes.

"Has everyone showered?" Ginny asked.

"Everyone but the little girls who are in the bathtub upstairs," Barbara answered.

"Good," Ginny said, putting down the plate in her hand. "My turn."

Brad and Mark turned to her. "You mean you haven't showered?" Mark asked.

"Not yet. But I will now. You two can clean the kitchen," she said sweetly over her shoulder as she left the room.

Ceely and Holly laughed. "You two always seem to avoid doing dishes. Ginny finally called you out," Ceely said laughing.

When Ginny had finished showering, she asked Adam if he had found any information about the power outage. He told her that her co-op bought energy from three sources, and that they had been able to get enough to bring the power back online. Unfortunately, the terrorists had bombed the steam plant on Lake Norman. Power from Royal Electric would not be dependable. Also, because so much of the grid had gone offline due to attacks on generating plants, power was being diverted to other areas. There were going to be intermittent blackouts for a while.

"I can live with that," Ginny said. "At least it isn't completely gone for good."

Later, Barbara approached Ginny in the kitchen and told her that Holly had helped her, Ceely, and Leah move the girls' air mattresses into the master suite. If the power went out in the middle of the night, they knew the girls would be frightened. This way Holly would be there to reassure them. Ginny nodded in understanding.

Pete was nearby and heard the conversation. When Barbara left, he approached Ginny.

"Did they do that without asking you?" Pete asked. "That's your room."

"They coordinated that with Holly," Ginny answered. "It's all right. I was going to suggest it. They just beat me to it."

"How are you going to get any sleep in a room with not only Holly, but three little girls?" he asked.

"I have one more roll away bed in the attic," Ginny said, looking thoughtful. "If it's hard to sleep, I'll set it up in the parlor. It will be fine."

"Ginny somehow this doesn't seem right," Pete said, running a hand through his hair and feeling annoyed. "This is your house. We're all piling in on you, and no one seems to realize you are being displaced. Brad too. Your siblings take you for granted way too much."

"Pete, I'm okay with it," Ginny said and reassuringly touched his arm. "I would rather be displaced with everyone here than be in my room worrying about my family if they weren't here."

Pete sighed and led Ginny to their usual evening spot on the porch. They settled into the swing, and Pete began to feel himself relax. In the evening twilight, the yard looked different. The tall game fence gave both a sense of security and a feeling of foreboding. Even Barf felt the difference as he climbed the steps to the porch, whining for attention. Ginny smiled as she scratched him behind the ears.

Ginny and Pete talked as the sun set. In the darkness he pulled her onto his lap and kissed her.

"Ginny Reed," Pete whispered, "do you know that I love you? I think I fell in love with you at the Greensboro Airport when you said I could come back to the farm with you."

"Peter Flinn," Ginny answered as she put her hand on his cheek, "do you know that I love you back? I think I felt it at the airport when I smiled at you and you smiled back at me."

Pete held her eyes with his.

"Will you marry me, Ginny?" he asked softly.

"Yes," she answered smiling. "I would love to marry you."

Pete kissed her. "When?"

"Whenever. We need to find a preacher," she said.

"Who's yours?" Pete asked.

"He lives in Elkin," Ginny explained. "He may not even be there. I think he moved here from another part of the state. Garrett is the resident pastor. We can ask him in the morning. It may not be a legal marriage since it's not registered at the courthouse, but it will be blessed. We can take care of the formalities later."

"Okay. That'll work," Pete said. "I don't have a ring for you."

"I have my mother's if that's okay with you," Ginny said.

"You have all the answers," Pete said as he grinned and began moving the swing again.

"No, I don't," Ginny answered, leaning back against him. She closed her eyes and felt the sway of the swing.

"What don't you know?" Pete asked.

"Which side of the bed to you like to sleep on," she answered.

Pete burst into laughter. He hugged his fiancé and kissed her deeply.

CHAPTER 32

APRIL 24

The next morning, Pete and Ginny were preparing breakfast. Neither one of them could stop smiling. They stole quick glances at each other and grinned with their hidden secret. When Pete could stand it no longer, he grabbed Ginny's hand, pulled her into the pantry closet and quickly kissed her. Ginny left the closet grinning.

Barbara walked into the kitchen. She saw Ginny smiling.

"What are you smiling so big about?" she asked as she poured a cup of coffee.

The others drifted towards the coffee pot, waiting their turn. When they heard Barbara's question, they looked at Ginny. Ginny looked at Pete who held the bag of coffee he had retreived from the pantry. He looked around the room and placed the bag on the counter.

"Well," Pete said, "I asked Ginny to marry me, and she said yes."

"Well, it's about time," Mark said dryly. "We've been waiting for that announcement. We aren't blind."

Then with a prearranged signal, everyone started fist bumping each other and laughing. Ginny blinked then blushed. Pete laughed and hugged her.

Everyone was talking at once, and Ginny whispered to Pete, "They were watching! This is so embarrassing."

Pete hugged her and said, "No, Babe. This is love and support. Embrace the moment."

Leah, who was sitting at the computer, suddenly stood and started shouting, "Be quiet!"

"What is it?" Mark asked as he quickly walked to the computer to look at the screen.

"Two people coming up the drive," Leah said, pointing to the monitor.

Mark and Pete looked at the computer. "Ginny, do you know those people?" Mark asked.

Ginny looked at the screen. Two small figures holding hands were walking up the driveway.

"Oh no!" she muttered, stepping back from the computer. "Those are the Miller kids. Something must be terribly wrong."

Ginny ran out the back door, through the gate at the new fence, and to the driveway where she met the children. Thomas, who was ten, was leading his little sister, Jordan, who was seven. Jordan was crying, and Ginny could tell that Thomas was trying hard not to.

"What happened, Thomas?" Ginny asked. The sight was confusing to her. The children were dressed appropriately, like nothing was wrong, but why were two children walking alone this early in the morning during a time of crisis?

"Somebody shot our dad," Thomas answered. His voice shook, and he blinked back tears before they could fall to his cheeks. "Mom had to take him to Elkin. She told us to come stay with you until they got back."

"When did this happen?" Mark asked. He had quietly come through the gate and was listening to the conversation.

"Last night. Dad was bleeding, and Mom needed to get him to the hospital. She locked us in the house, and we waited until the sun came up to come here. It's not that far to walk. Is it okay if we're here?" Thomas asked.

"One hundred percent okay, Thomas," Ginny said gently. "Have you had breakfast?"

The children shook their heads no.

"Well, come inside," Ginny said, leading them through the gate and across the backyard. "We're eating now. Do you want cereal or pancakes?"

"Pancakes," the two said.

"I thought you looked like pancake lovers," Ginny said, smiling as she opened the back door. "I am too, that's how I know. Come with me." Ginny sat the children at the kitchen table with plates of pancakes and syrup. As fast as they ate, Ginny wondered when their last meal had been.

Just as the children were finishing their meal, Riley, Haley, and Geeta came down the stairs and into the kitchen. They stopped when they saw Jordan and Thomas.

"Girls," Ginny said, "come here and meet Jordan and Thomas. They will be spending the day here while their parents are in Elkin. Why don't you take Jordan with you to check on the chickens."

"Sure," Riley said. "Come on, Jordan. I'm Riley, that's Haley, and that's Geeta. Where are your parents?"

"At the hospital," Jordan said softly as she got up from the table. "My daddy got hurt." Ginny noticed the little girl's lower lip tremble slightly.

"Oh, well, then he'll be all right," Riley said. "Hospitals always fix people."

Jordan's trembling lip turn into a slight smile. Ginny grinned. Leave it to children to comfort each other.

Caleb and Bobby ran up the stairs from the basement and started to go out the back door.

"Caleb," Ginny called.

The boys stopped and turned around. "Yes ma'am?" Caleb asked.

"Boys, this is Thomas," Ginny said as she put her arm around the boy. "He's staying with us today until his parents get back from Elkin. Can he hang out with you?"

"Sure." Caleb said. "Come on, Thomas. We have some chores to do outside. You can help." Thomas got up and followed Caleb and Bobby.

As Ginny got up to rejoin the adults at the dining room table, her phone rang.

"This is Dr. Reed." When Ginny heard the voice on the other end of the phone, she exclaimed, "Lacy! I'm so glad you're okay. How's Hank?"

"He's going to survive," Lacy said as she looked at her husband lying in the hospital bed, an IV slowly adding fluids to his body, "but he will be here probably two more days." Lacy paused, "Ginny he lost a lot of blood, and the hospital doesn't have any. They barely have IV fluids. They can't get the quantity of supplies like they used to, and no one is donating blood. Half the staff doesn't show up for work, and the ones here are overworked. I had no idea it would be like this here.

"Wow," Ginny said softly as she sat on a stool at the kitchen island, "that sounds awful, but I"m glad Hank's going to get well. The kids made it here."

"Ginny," Lacy said, "I feel just awful about that. It was dark, and I needed to get Hank to the hospital. I locked the kids inside and told them to walk to your house when the sun came up and they could see the way without using a flashlight. I would never do that unless it was an emergency."

"Lacy, I know," Ginny said as she leaned forward with her hand on her head, elbows propped on the island. "These are not normal times. No judgement, I promise. You made the right call telling them to come here. It's not far, and they waited until daylight. Don't worry about them. They can stay with us for as long as they need to, no worries.

I'll take them to your house to get clothes. Lacy, did you see who shot Hank?"

"Yes," Lacy said angrily as she stood up and moved to the window. "It was Dwight Hall."

"What was he doing?" Ginny asked.

"He was sneaking past the house toward the pasture," Lacy replied. "He triggered the motion sensor lights. By the time Hank got outside with his shotgun, Dwight was already in the pasture and separating a small heifer from the herd. Hank yelled at him to stop. Dwight just shot him. Hank hadn't even aimed his gun." Lacy paused, and Ginny heard her voice shake, "I'd rather lose the whole herd than Hank."

"I know, Lacy," Ginny said sadly. "Hank's life is priceless. I'm not surprised it's Dwight Hall. He's the one behind all the thefts. I'll tell Brad. He can call the sheriff."

"No need," Lacy said. "It's already been reported."

After reassuring Lacy again that the children were safe, Ginny ended the call and placed her phone on the island with a deep, but relieved sigh.

Mark had come into the kitchen during Ginny's phone call.

"Was that their mom?" he asked.

"Yes," she answered. "Hank will live, but he'll be in the hospital a couple days. The kids will stay here. Lacy said it was Dwight Hall. The hospital has already reported him."

"I'm not surprised," Mark said with a sad sigh. "It's only been three days since Pete and Bennett caught him in our pasture. He must be desperate. Well, lazy, too." He turned to go out the back door. "I'll tell Brad he doesn't have to worry about contacting the sheriff."

Ginny nodded and went outside to reassure Thomas that his father was going to recover. Then she went to find the girls so she could tell Jordan the good news.

After lunch, Mark and Pete introduced a stricter security plan.

Loaded rifles and shotguns were placed on the inside wall above the outside doors, out of the reach of the smaller children. The teens were given specific doors and windows to lock if an alarm sounded, then they were to to take the children downstairs to the storage room. The adults were given locations to guard and shoot from if necessary.

Bennett pulled his truck into the driveway just inside the game fence and parked it. He would stand behind the truck's door and talk to the people and turn them away if possible. If not, he would signal the others inside the house. The group was quiet as each one processed the possibility that they might have to defend their home and children.

After the assignments were made, Mark held a few drills so everyone could get used to the tasks for which they were responsible. Ginny and Erica were given the responsibility of prepositioning supplies to quickly set up a treatment area for anyone wounded, but they were to carry firearms in a holster.

After the drill Ginny went to see Bennett.

"Show me your truck," she said. "I want to see how you can protect yourself."

Bennett opened the door and explained that the windows, windshield, and all the metal were reinforced and bullet proof. Then he showed her the panels at the bottom of the door that dropped down to protect his feet and legs.

"This is amazing," she said. "But what made you do this?"

"The things I saw in the marines. I saw things in other countries that would give even the bravest person nightmares. It takes less than you might think for a seemingly civilized country to fall into chaos. Having seen that firsthand, I decided to be prepared after I left the marines. One of the first things I did was have my truck customized." He pointed to case of grenades sitting on the passenger seat. "I picked these up as soon as those missiles were launched. It would take one of those to stop this truck. I have them to lob over the fence if necessary."

"You are one scary dude," Ginny said, shaking her head and looking out at a pasture. Looking back at him, she said, "I'm glad I can call you a friend, and I'm glad you're here."

"You're pretty awesome yourself, Doc," Bennett said as he laughed at her description of him. "The way you patch up people, I'm glad I can call you a friend, too." He sobered, "Thank you for letting me stay with your family and with Heather and her family. I'm glad I'm here, too."

The two walked back to the house to start their chores for the day.

CHAPTER 33

APRIL 25

After breakfast, the clean-up crew was working on the kitchen and setting out cookware for lunch. The other adults were sitting around the dining room table discussing their activities for the day. Brett was sitting at the computer.

"Motorcycles coming up from the south!" he yelled, "and they're turning into our driveway!"

Mark sounded the alarm. Adults gathered the children and sent them downstairs. Teens ran through the house locking doors and windows that would be unattended. Men and women gathered their guns and took their places at designated windows. Adam replaced Brett at the computer so Brett and Michael could launch Brett's drone. Bennett ran to his truck and stood behind its open door.

Adam watched the computer screen as the motorcyclists pulled up the rebar and cut the wire that had been stretched across the driveway. Then four motorcyclists and a truck slowly approached the house. They stopped at the fence.

The leader of the gang was short. His limp hair was probably light brown, but it was dark with dirt and oil. He wore jeans that rode low on his hips, and a t-shirt stretched over his abdomen, which folded over his belt. He got off his bike and walked to the fence. The other members of the gang stayed on their bikes and in the truck.

"How can I help you boys?" Bennett asked. He was standing between the cab of his truck and the open door. His arms were draped casually across the frame of the door, but his rifle was within easy reach.

"We want the doc," the leader answered arrogantly.

"What doc?" Bennett asked.

"Doc Reed, the vet," the leader said impatiently. He pointed to the house, "She lives here."

"Why?" Bennett asked calmly.

"We need her."

"Why?" Bennett asked again.

The leader of the group sighed and looked around the yard and the pasture, signaling his growing impatience. Then he looked directly at Bennett.

"We have a large compound just off 421," the man said. "We're farming everything with horses. We need a vet to take care of them. We also have some guys who need stitching up," he said, giving Bennett a pointed look. "She can do that, too."

"You'll have to find another one," Bennett said. "Doc Reed doesn't want to come with you."

"Why don't you let her speak for herself?" the man asked.

"I don't have to. I know her mind," Bennett answered.

The leader looked at the house and the property around it.

"All right, Big Man. Have it your way, but we'll be back, and you won't like what's coming. But if you let the Doc come with us, we'll leave you alone. We might even set up some trades. You think about it. We'll be seeing you."

The motorcyclists headed slowly back down the driveway and disappeared into the trees between the house and the road. The truck turned around and followed them off the property. When they were gone, Bennett walked back into the house.

"What did they want?" asked Mark. "We couldn't hear much."

Bennett scanned the room. His eyes landed on the children, who had come back upstairs and were huddled around the door to the basement. They looked unsure and a little frightened. Bennett looked at Mark and nodded toward them.

"Bonnie," Mark said, "will you and Hannah take the little ones back downstairs?"

"Sure," Bonnie replied. "Come on guys, what will it be this time?" As her voice faded down the stairs, the adults heard her say, "Sorry, Riley, it's the boys' turn to pick an activity."

Everyone looked back at Bennett.

"They wanted Ginny."

"What?" Mark exclaimed, looking shocked.

"Why?" Pete asked with a low, angry voice. He stood protectively beside Ginny.

"They evidently have developed a large compound of people just off Highway 421," Bennett answered. "Either their machines won't work or they ran out of gas, because they're farming with horses. They must have a lot. They want Ginny to go back with them to care for the livestock."

"Are some sick or injured?" Ginny asked.

"He didn't say," Bennett answered, "but, Ginny, if you go, you won't be coming back. They won't let you. The leader said if you went with them, they would leave us alone, even trade with us, which I doubt they'll do. They look like the type of men that take what they want without asking. You can't go. I don't think you would be mistreated because you have a skill they need, but your life would be miserable."

"If I don't, what will happen?" Ginny asked.

"They're coming back," Bennett answered. "I don't know when, but there will be more of them."

"If I can save everyone here," Ginny said, looking at Mark, "I'll have to go. There's no choice."

"Of course you have a choice, Ginny," Mark said. "Those people are stupid. They told us their intentions, and that gives us time to prepare. Bennett, Alex, Pete, and I will come up with a plan. Trust us, Ginny. You won't be going with them."

"All right," she said. "What are we doing?"

"Give us thirty minutes to plan," Mark said, "and then we'll get started."

Mark, Pete, Bennett, and Alex, gathered around the dining room table and began discussing options to deter the motorcyclists. Garrett, Robert, and Brad joined them. They drew diagrams and made lists. Garrett called Brett over and began asking him questions.

Finally, thirty minutes later, Mark stood up.

"We have a plan," he said.

Mark explained that incendiary bombs would be placed in the trees then ignited and dropped using a remote control. Wire would be placed on remote controlled, spring-loaded traps to fly up and hit the motorcyclists in the chest or neck. If that didn't stop them, Bennett would launch grenades over the fence from a second story window using a modified sling shot. Also, every room would have an adult with a firearm at an open window.

A crucial part of the plan was moving food and clothes to the house Brad had bought from the Thompsons. The goal was to have two changes of clothes for every person. Plus, most of the nonperishable food would be transferred there. The children would be taken to the house as soon as supplies were moved.

That afternoon, everything was in place, and an early dinner was served. Everyone ate the meatloaf and vegetables that had been cooked. The smaller children in the breakfast nook were joking and laughing as usual, but the teens and adults sat quietly eating, nervous tension thick in the air.

After dinner, Brad helped Heather, Robert, and Leah settle the children at his house then returned.

Ginny kept herself busy with cleaning the kitchen and folding laundry. Her hands trembled slightly, and she felt her heart pounding in her chest. Pete came over, took her by the hand and led her out to the backyard where they sat in two of the lawn chairs.

The late afternoon sun cast cooling shadows over the yard. A breeze brought the scent of peonies mixed with pine. The chickens were fussing over scraps from dinner, and Barf was digging at a mole track beside the equipment shed.

"It's so quiet with the children gone," Ginny said as she watched Barf. "They should be out here playing tag or hide and seek."

"It's going to be all right, Ginny," Pete reassured her and took her hand. "This is a good plan. Those guys were street thugs who think we are stupid hicks. That's to our advantage. They will underestimate us. If they were smart, they would've asked for the farmer in residence to come as well. If they can't take care of their animals, they probably can't grow food, either." Pete held her tight when he felt her start to shake.

"I've never been so scared, Pete," Ginny said, looking up at him. Pete's calm eyes began to give her strength. "I have never felt like someone wanted to hurt me before all this or exploit my skills. I can't bear the possibility of anyone here getting hurt because of me. That's the worst part."

Pete raised her face to his and kissed her.

"I love you, Ginny Reed. Remember that. Take strength from that, and take strength that God as a plan."

Pete held Ginny's hand as the two sat in silence. A few minutes later, they heard voices behind the campers. It was Donna and Aaron.

"Aaron, this isn't our fight," they heard Donna say in a trembling voice. "Let's leave and go back to the barn. We can take Carson, Grace and the girls. We don't have to risk our lives here."

"No, Donna," Aaron replied firmly. "You forget they risked their lives for us first. If Pete and Bennett hadn't come to our house that day, I would be dead, and Bonnie would be who knows where. This is not a one-way street, Donna. These people have taken us in and shared everything they have. I won't hear another word about leaving."

They could hear Donna crying.

"Please Aaron." Donna cried harder.

"Donna, I know you're scared," Aaron said. "We all are, but you can't abandon the people who helped you first. I'm going back in. You stay here and collect yourself. I don't want anyone to suspect you are so frightened you're ready to bail on them."

Aaron walked around the camper; anger was evident in his walk and clenched fists. He stopped abruptly when he saw Pete and Ginny in the yard.

He sighed, "I'm sorry. I know you heard that. She's scared."

"It's all right, Aaron," Ginny said. "I'm scared, too. I think what Donna wants to do is only natural. Don't be too hard on her."

"You're a good person, Ginny," Aaron said. "Thank you."

CHAPTER 34

APRIL 25

Ginny and Pete watched Aaron walk into the house. Donna went into the camper shared by Grace and the girls. They could hear Grace comforting and reassuring her sister. Not wanting to eavesdrop, they turned toward the house. The late afternoon sun cast their long shadows across the yard, and they heard a commotion inside.

Erica, who was watching the computers, yelled, "Motorcycles coming from the south. Slowing to come into the drive."

Pete and Ginny ran into the house. Adults were running to their posts and checking their weapons. Adam took Erica's place at the computer. Ginny and Erica cleared a portable table in the dining room and covered it with a water proof drape. Then they laid out supplies on the dining room table.

"Everyone in place!" Mark yelled.

From the upstairs window, Brad could see four trucks and about a dozen motorcycles. He reported to Mark. Adam confirmed the count from the computer screen. On a walkie talkie, Michael also confirmed the report from the drone display. He and Brett were standing behind the equipment shed.

"Not as many as I feared," Mark, who was standing at the window in the parlor, said to Pete, who was at the front window in his room. "This will be easier than we thought."

The trucks and motorcycles stopped in the drive at the fence and shut off their engines. Suddenly, everything was so quiet the cows could be heard mooing nervously in the pastures.

The leader got off his motorcycle. He was taller than the man who had spoken that morning. He wore dirty jeans and a black leather vest with no shirt. His abdomen was large and folded over his belt like a blob. A tattoo of a dagger dripping with blood covered his right upper arm, and silver knife earrings dangled from his pierced earlobes.

"Let us have the Doc," the man called out arrogantly and condescendingly, like he was explaining what he wanted to a child.

Mark spoke into a radio. The receiver was at the fence.

"No. Go home."

The leader turned and loudly said in a voice that sounded both enthusiastic and ominous, "All right boys. Game time. This is going to be fun."

His words made Ginny sick to her stomach. She could tell by their twisted smiles that these were cruel men. Bennett had been right. She watched as the incendiary bombs were ignited in the trees and released burning oil and gasoline on the trucks and motorcyclists in the back of the group. Alex had the control at an upstairs window. She didn't know how he had the courage to press the button, because the sight of men on fire, the smell of fire and burning flesh, and the screams of the men were something she would never forget.

The leader ignored the chaos behind him as he quickly snipped through the fence wire with bolt cutters. He pulled the fence back and came across the yard. A shot sounded from the second story, and he dropped to the ground dead, shot through the head. Others stormed through the hole in the fence. It was easy to tell that they were angry.

Gun fire erupted from the upstairs windows. Bullets rained down onto the ground below. Some hit their marks, and some sprayed dirt and grass into the air. The men on the ground fired back, and she could hear the sound of breaking glass in the windows and bullets hitting the outside of her house. Fortunately for her family, the men in the yard were killed before they could reach the porch.

The gang members who were still outside the fence were trapped. The trucks and motorcycles on fire blocked the driveway so their escape route was impassable. Two ran toward the woods. Gunshot sounded, and they fell, dead. Then all was quiet except for the crackling of the fires that lit the vehicles and the yard and woods around them. She saw movement behind one of the motorcycles, and two men fired from the woods. She heard a scream upstairs. Someone had been injured. Gun fire came from the second story windows, and the two men dropped to the ground. No one moved.

"Hold your positions," Ginny heard Mark shout.

"I've got pressure on Garrett's wound!" Barbara called. "We're bringing him downstairs.

Ginny's heart pounded, and she wanted to cry. Garrett must have been shot. She quickly started opening supplies as she heard Garrett and Barbara coming down the stairs.

Ginny turned to go to the stairs to help when she felt a hand across her mouth tight enough that she knew she would bruise. She felt an arm around her waist that pulled her back against a man's hard chest. Ginny felt herself gag at the smell of sweat and body odor.

Ginny struggled and bit her teeth into the man's hand. He yelped and released her. Ginny shoved her elbow into his stomach. He bent over, which allowed her to step away from him. The sound brought Pete from the parlor. The invader saw Pete and raised a gun.

Standing by the dining room table, only a couple feet from the biker, Ginny screamed.

"No!" she shouted and lunged for the man's arm. The biker fired at Pete.

CHAPTER 35

APRIL 5

Ginny sat straight up in her bed, the gutteral, panicked scream she let out woke her. Brad heard her. He jumped out of bed, ran down the hall and entered her room.

"What is it?" he asked, sounding out of breath. "Are you all right? Did you have a nightmare?"

Ginny rubbed her eyes and pushed her hair back from her face. The shadowy light of dawn filtered through her bedroom window, giving her the ability to look around her room. Still disoriented, she looked at her watch, checking the date as well as the time.

"Yes," she said. "I can't believe the detail of the dream I just had. It was awful. The country was attacked. The government collapsed, and a bunch of us were here trying to survive."

"Wait, you had that dream?" Brad asked incredulously.

"Yes, why?"

"I had the same one. How can that be?" he asked.

"Maybe the salad dressing at supper had gone bad," Ginny said. "Maybe we saw the same news report. I don't know. I do know I won't be able to fall back to sleep. I'm getting up."

"Me too, I guess," Brad said.

The two sat at the breakfast nook picking at their food.

"Let's talk about this," Brad said, dropping his fork on his plate. "I'll tell you what I dreamed. Then you tell me what you dreamed."

As Brad described his dream, Ginny felt her jaw drop at the similarities.

"Brad," she said, "that's basically the same dream I had. What do you think?"

"I'm glad the transaction with the Thompson's is over, and I think I'm going to go buy farm supplies," he answered. "The corn can wait."

"Do you think we should do that?" Ginny asked.

"Yes," Brad said emphatically. "Ginny, the Bible says that men will dream dreams. This has to be a sign."

Ginny nodded, "I'll order a bunch of medical supplies and have them overnighted. Today is April 5. My trip is in five days. If I go to the airport and see people that were in my dream, I will be convinced and terrified."

They were discussing plans when Brad's phone rang.

"Mark! How are you?" Brad answered then started listening. Finally he said, "Sure, you know your family is always wecome here, even if it isn't an emergency. Why?" Brad listened for a moment. "Mark, stop. I'm going to put you on speaker. Ginny's here."

Brad put his phone in the speaker mode and placed it on the table.

"Now," Brad said, "tell me again with Ginny listening."

Mark detailed a dream he had just before waking up.

"It has me spooked," he said. "Can I position some supplies there just in case?"

"Yes," Brad answered, "but you have to know that Ginny and I had that same dream."

"Are you kidding? That's crazy!" Mark exclaimed. "I don't know what to make of this."

Ginny's phone rang. Her screen showed Garrett's picture.

"Garrett! How are you?" she answered. Ginny listened then said, "Wait, I'm going to put you on speaker." Ginny placed her phone beside Brad's.

"Garrett, Brad's phone is on speaker with Mark on the other end. Tell them what you told me."

Garrett told his siblings about his dream.

"This is unbelieveable," Brad said. "We all had the same dream. This can't be a coincidence. This is a God thing. He's giving us a chance to get ready."

"I agree," Garrett said. "The question is, why is He giving us this warning. My dream didn't reveal that."

"Neither did ours," Ginny said.

"Nor mine," Mark said.

Garrett said, "I say we plan. We position supplies ahead of time. We had the same people in the dreams. I can't imagine they wouldn't be a part of this."

The four siblings divided the list of medical supplies, nonperishable food, and survival gear. Finally, they agreed to meet that evening at the farm to make more plans.

By Sunday afternoon, the basement storage area, storage sheds, and equipment shed were full of food, weapons, ammunition, toiletries, cleaning materials, lumber, tools and the extra medical supplies.

The four sat around the breakfast nook trying to think of what they may have forgotten.

"I guess we're as ready as we can be," Garrett said. "Barbara is packing what's left at the house. We're staying in Winston tonight just in case none of this happens, but we're keeping the kids out of school just in case it does."

"Same," Mark said. "I called Mike, Ceely's brother. He had a more limited dream and a sense of foreboding he couldn't explain. The same with Heather's brother, Bennett. They're getting prepared as well."

"The same with Robert," Garrett said. "He's putting off a trip out of town until after tomorrow."

"Tomorrow," Ginny said nervously. "Tomorrow will let us know if we're crazy or blessed."

"Well, I need to get going," Mark said, standing up. "I have an hour's drive home and I'm tired. I'm hoping that this time tomorrow we can call ourselves crazy."

"Me too," Garrett chimed as he stood to leave.

"Be careful," Ginny called after them.

CHAPTER 36

APRIL 10

Ginny's alarm sounded, but she was already awake and dressed. She took her carry-on bag downstairs and placed it by the back door. After pouring herself a cup of coffee, Ginny turned on the television, and tried to eat some breakfast. She felt so nervous that she could barely swallow.

Turning to Brad, Ginny said, "The news seems just like typical news. Spring weather, complaints about the politicians, stock market advice, global issues. Part of me will feel foolish if this doesn't happen, but most of me is hoping I get the chance to feel foolish."

Ginny looked at her watch.

"Time to go." She paused. "I know I could just stay here and call the pet food company, but if none of this happens, I'll make the trip. Also, I want to make sure Pete, Alex, and Erica get here safely."

"I understand," Brad said thoughtfully. "I think you're doing the right thing. Just be careful."

Brad picked up her bag and walked her to the truck. Ginny placed it in the cab and turned to hug Brad.

"Stay safe," Brad said as Ginny climbed into the driver's seat and he closed her door.

Ginny started the engine and pulled into the driveway to begin the trip to the airport. When she looked into the rearview mirror, she felt amazed that the farm looked just like it had in her dream.

Getting through security was easy, and Ginny made her way to the first class lounge. She was grateful that the Pure Pet Food Company had given her a first-class ticket; otherwise, she would not have met Pete and Alex in the dream. Ginny opened the door and went in.

Alex was not holding the door for her, and Pete was not sitting in the back row, which disappointed her. Unsure how to feel, Ginny got a bottle of water from the hostess. She decided to just wait and see what happened. When she turned around, she found Alex Freeman standing behind her and smiling.

"Ginny Reed?" he asked.

"Alex Freeman?"

Alex pulled her to the side. "Did you have the same dream?"

"I must have if you're asking me about it," she answered. "Brad, Mark and Garrett did too, but Mark felt like he wasn't suppose to contact you."

"Exactly!" Alex said. "Pete and I felt like we weren't supposed to contact you, either. It's like this moment was to happen this way to prove we had been warned."

The changing monitors caught their eyes. Part of the flights had been delayed or cancelled, and the televisions had stopped regular programming.

Ginny felt her stomach clench and her chest tightened with anxiety. "This is really happening, isn't it?"

"Come with me," Alex said.

"Can you leave?" Ginny asked.

Alex grinned. "I changed my shift. I just got off. We'll take the back way out. I'll take you to your truck."

Ginny got into Alex's SUV which was loaded with supplies. He drove Ginny to her truck.

"Follow me," he said. "You may know the way, but just in case."

Ginny grinned, "Lead on."

Ginny pulled into the apartment complex behind Alex. Erica stood on the sidewalk next to her sedan, which was also loaded with supplies. She hugged Ginny.

"I knew you would come," she said.

"You had the dream, too?" asked Ginny.

"Me too," Erica answered.

"And me too," a deep voice said behind them.

Ginny heard the voice. She looked around, and there stood a tall man with dark hair and dark eyes. She was stunned. It was Pete.

"Don't I get a hug, too?" he asked.

Ginny needed no encouragement; she launched herself into Pete's arms. Pete hugged her and kissed her hard.

"I already know I love you," he whispered.

"I know. I love you too," Ginny whispered back, not trying to hide her smile.

"I want to introduce you to some people who weren't in the dream," Pete said then stepped to the side. He introduced her to two of his friends who were also highly trained employees, Max Benton and Sharon Ingram.

"Nice to meet you," Ginny said, shaking their hands. "Welcome to the farm."

"We've already made changes to the dream, Pete!" Ginny exclaimed as she looked at him. "Alex changed his shift. You brought friends. We're all better supplied. We don't have to have the same outcome as what we dreamed! We can be better, safer!"

Ginny laughed when Pete held up his fist for their characteristic fist bump. She felt a sense of hope as she looked at the people who were already her friends because of a dream.

"Let's go home," she said.

The group formed a caravan with Ginny in the lead. The early morning sun was behind them as they left Oak Ridge. It felt like the sun and wind were at their backs, easing their way west and giving them hope for a better future than what might have been without the dream, which they all believed had been a gift from God.

Look for "Second Chances," the second book of the Forewarned Series. The Reed family and their friends struggle to adapt to the new world they are facing. They are constantly amazed at how accurate the dreams were and at how the dreams are being changed in both good and bad ways. Also, the conspiracy behind the bombs is revealed.

Also by A. K. Gentry

<u>Whitlow Series</u>
An Awkward Inheritance, Book 1
An Unlikely Partnership, Book 2
An Unforeseen Danger, Book 3

The Perfect Loophole

ABOUT THE AUTHOR

A. K. Gentry is a writer of Christian Fiction. Having grown up in rural North Carolina, she has lived around farms and small towns her whole life. She brings her love of rural living and Christian values to her writing.

Gentry is a retired registered nurse. Her immediate family consists of her husband, two daughters, one son-in-law, two granddaughters, and two grand-dogs. She is also blessed with an extended family who bring a richness to life for which she is grateful.